Wh

"THE ARRI___ MW01048309 ᴇnes were sizzling hot and graphic, but well penned and creative, and deserving of its NC-17 rating. Hysterically funny during other scenes, THE ARRIVAL also boasts some suspenseful moments. As far as I'm concerned, this story has all the elements I look forward to in a romantic fantasy, so I happily recommend it to all."

- Astrid Kinn, Romance Reviews Today

Also by Jordan Summers

- Tears of Amun

Discover for yourself why readers can't get enough of the multiple award-winning publisher Ellora's Cave. Whether you prefer e-books or paperbacks, be sure to visit EC on the web at www.ellorascave.com for an erotic reading experience that will leave you breathless.

www.ellorascave.com

Ellora's Cave Publishing, Inc.

PO Box 787

Hudson, OH 44236-0787

ISBN # 1-84360-568-6

Warrior, 2003.

ALL RIGHTS RESERVED

Ellora's Cave Publishing, Inc.

© Atlanean's Quest 1: The Arrival, Jordan Summers, 2003.

This book may not be reproduced in whole or in part without author and publisher permission.

Edited by Jennifer Martin.

Cover art by Christine Clavel.

Warning: The following material contains strong sexual content meant for mature readers. *ATLANEAN'S QUEST I: THE ARRIVAL* has been rated NC17 erotic, by a minimum of three independent reviewers. We strongly suggest storing this book in a place where young readers not meant to view it are unlikely to happen upon it. That said, enjoy…

ATLANTEAN'S QUEST I: THE ARRIVAL

Written by

JORDAN SUMMERS

Acknowledgements:

To Si:

Thank you for being everything that I never knew I wanted.

How do you thank your parents? You don't. I love you Mom and Dad & Mum and Dad. 'T' thanks for being a great sister. And to the better half of T-n-T thanks for all the laughs you've brought to my life. And finally, last but not least, I'd like to thank Jen for all her hard work and dedication.

Prologue

The jungle air was thick and repressive, palpable to the taste. Like a living entity it vibrated and pulsed with an energy all its own. Animal cries rang out as predator met prey in a violent exchange that played out night after night.

A small pot set in a clearing boiled with pungent herbs and the flesh of the mighty anaconda. Steam hissed, thick fumes of smoke bellowed, wood burned, popping as each piece of kindling was snatched up by the ravenous flame.

The woman, known as Ariel the seer, stood over the crackling fire stirring the contents of the pot. Visible through the sheer material of her earthen skirt, firm muscles in her lithe legs strained. Sweat beaded her delicate brow.

With each swirling pass of the spoon, Ariel's ample breasts bobbed. Rose-colored nipples marbled from exposure to the warm night air, begging to be caressed and suckled. Long blonde hair fell in loose waves around her trim waist and over her rounded hips. Her aqua gaze fell trancelike upon the brew in search of the elusive vision.

Eros stood to the side of the seer, his massive arms crossed over his wide hairless chest, expanding his biceps to inhuman proportions. He'd braided his blond hair in the ceremonial custom of his people, divided into two plaits that fell to the small of his back. His breathing was even, despite the nervous energy coursing through his muscle-corded body, as he waited for the seer's vision to form.

Ariel gestured for Eros to come forward. Tonight the medicine must be stronger. I need your seed to add to the brew.

The words came into his head on a whisper. Such was the way of Atlantean communication. Unquestioning, Eros untied his loincloth, allowing it to fall away from his trim waist and thick thighs.

The night air taunted like a dream-lover's caress, promising much, delivering little. A faint breeze spilled over his rod, rustling the crisp curls that grew at the base. He reached down to take himself in hand, but the seer stopped his movement with a light touch of her fingertips.

I must be the one who brings your seed forth this night, for the ritual to be complete.

Eros nodded and dropped his hands to his sides. The seer stepped forward and cupped his heavy sac in her soft palms, transferring his weight back and forth until balance was achieved. Her gentle touch brought forth the desired results. His staff hardened, lengthening to its full ten inches within seconds.

At once, she slipped to her knees impaling her mouth with his throbbing cock. Her lips were hot, moist, made for giving pleasure. He sucked in a breath, but said nothing. Ariel began swirling her tongue around the head of his staff, like she'd done so many times before when he'd sought relief. Her hands gently massaged his balls, supping at him as if he were her first meal after a long starvation.

Eros gave his body up to the pleasurable sensation and closed his eyes, imagining what it would feel like to thrust into his future mate. Like a siren of the sea, the warmth of the seer's mouth urged, beckoned, and lured the seed from him. He felt his sac draw up as Ariel added pressure and switched to sucking, sliding her hand up and down his thick cock.

As he started to ejaculate, Ariel pulled away, ensuring he spilled his essence into the strange mixture bubbling within the pot. Eros jerked as the last of his fluids were milked from his body.

Ariel returned to the pot and stirred a couple more times. Her eyes intense, focused, waiting.

Excitement filled her mind, spilling over into Eros. *She comes, my King. Her arrival heralds the new dawn of our people.*

Eros lowered his gaze in respect. *Are you certain?* He normally never questioned the seer, yet tonight he had no choice. Her vision must be true.

For his sake. For the sake of his people.

Ariel hesitated, clearing the smoke from around the gurgling pot with a wave of her slender hand. *'Tis true. She will arrive within seven moonrises. 'Tis more than enough time to bring her here and perform the mating ritual. Remember, you must not join with her until the ceremony has been completed.*

Aye, he answered silently.

Wait. She stilled, her eyes widened a bit and her breath caught. *You must use caution, for she does not travel alone.*

Eros stiffened, rage coursing through his body. *Do you see her with a mate?*

The seer's mouth held the trace of a smile. His heart pounded painfully against his ribcage. It should not matter to him whether the woman had chosen a mate, but the ice forming in his veins said it did.

Nay. Ariel shook her head. But she is in danger from one who is very near.

His stomach clenched. His hands fisted so tight he half expected to hear bones breaking. *I will not allow any harm to come to her.*

Eros raised his head to the heavens. After all the waiting, his mate was finally coming. He had almost given up hope. But tonight Ariel had seen her. He could barely believe his good fortune.

Soon, he too would lay eyes on his future mate. Until then, there was much to do.

All is as it should be. Eros looked into the seer's face and nodded. *You have done your part, now 'tis time for me to do mine. Be well, Ariel the seer.* He dropped to his knees before her, kissing each bare nipple reverently as was custom, then rose and slipped into the darkness.

Be well, my King.

* * * * *

Rachel was back in the jungle—naked. Monkeys chattered and parrots screeched as she lay on a soft bed of grass in the small clearing. The blades tickled her bottom and stroked her shoulders as a breeze gently rustled them. Water gurgled and splashed playfully in the background, calling out for those around to join in its merriment. She considered answering its call, but she couldn't seem to sit up. The smell of exotic orchids wafted on the breeze, perfuming the air, bathing her skin with their luscious scent.

Suddenly all sound stopped. Even the leaves refused to whisper.

Rachel's heart began to pound, a combination of excitement and fear. Her rosy nipples stabbed skyward.

He was here.

Silent footfalls heralded his approach. Shadows from the trees shifted like a mirage as he strode toward her. Flawlessly muscled, his body chiseled perfection.

Rachel gasped and tried to get a glimpse of his face, but before she could do so, a strange shadowy light filtered over him obscuring his features.

She knew she should scream, but the sight of this stranger's body and his mammoth cock made her mouth water, her legs tremble, and her pussy ache.

It had been far too long since she'd had a man, and she *wanted* this one, more than she wanted her next breath. She raised her arms to reach for him, but he pulled back.

Rachel cursed.

The man kneeled between her thighs and pressed them apart, exposing her pussy. The shadows around his face refused to budge. He lowered his head and lapped at her swollen folds. Every nerve ending came alive, as his seeking tongue sent shockwaves through her body. She was already wet. A thin sheen of perspiration broke out on her skin, her nipples puckered even tighter until they ached. Rachel moaned, low and deep—animal-like.

Fuck me, please, she begged in her mind as she attempted to shift her hips.

He did not answer.

She heard his labored breath as he rose and positioned the head of his great cock at her entrance. He smelled of earth, spice and sex incarnate. A heady human aphrodisiac of male testosterone and primal urges. Rachel bucked her hips, nudging, encouraging, and pleading for his thick length. Didn't he realize how much she needed him?

He groaned. His large frame shook as if grasping for control.

She felt the pain-pressure as he started to push the tip of his thick erection inside, stretching her body beyond its limits. The moisture from her channel eased his way. Rachel whimpered, trying to find the words to ask for what she needed, but before a single syllable was uttered he vanished.

"Noooo!" The scream died on Rachel's lips as she jackknifed up in her bed. She blinked a couple of times and her apartment came into focus. Her body was drenched and her breathing ragged. The sheets were twisted around her ankles, effectively binding her to the bed. She looked around her studio apartment. The man was gone and her clit ached.

She'd been having the same erotic dream every night for the past month. Shadowy, elusive — downright frustrating, like the man in it. Rachel snorted and shook her head. She thought about him as if he were real.

She kicked the covers away and threw her legs over the side of the bed. Rachel padded into the bathroom, her bare feet echoing off the hardwood floors. There was no way she could go back to sleep without a good orgasm.

The buzz of her vibrator and her own soft moans rang out in the night's silence as she brought herself to climax while she imagined being fucked by the jungle god.

Chapter One

The restaurant in the Metropolitan Museum hummed with conversation. The day was brilliant. Light filtered in from the skylights, dappling the patron's faces as they devoured the delicacies before them.

Rachel Evans, Jaclyn Ward, and Brigit Taylor sat huddled in a corner, their chairs turned away from the throng, successfully closing out the masses.

"Are you sure you want to go through with this?" Jaclyn asked, her voice deceptively cool.

"Absolutely." Rachel took another bite of salad, chewing the crisp greens. "This is the opportunity of a lifetime."

Jaclyn picked up a pickle from her plate. Making a face close to revulsion, she placed the spear on Rachel's plate. Rachel laughed and lifted it up in front of her, like a conductor holding a baton. She stared at the pickle for a second. The veggie was firm and stiff, dripping with juices.

Visions of her dream man's massive cock flooded her mind. She bit down on her tongue to keep from moaning aloud. Her nipples tightened beneath her cotton shirt, making each scrape of the material exquisite torture. She took a bite of the pickle, sending its tart juices squirting into her mouth. Closing her eyes for a second in ecstasy, she murmured, "Mmm — I love dill pickles."

"Pickles. Riiight..." Jaclyn laughed, throwing her blonde head back. "You could have fooled me. That face you're making looks more like a woman having an orgasm than eating lunch."

Jaclyn pursed her lips in thought and toyed with the potato salad on her plate. "I think you need a good stiff dick inside you — the larger the better — instead of traipsing into the jungle. Say the word and I'll open my little black book and make a call."

Rachel's eyes widened as Jac flipped open her palm pilot and slipped the stylus from its holder. Jac methodically went down her address list, throwing out names. "Brett — now there's a cock a woman can sink onto — mmm...mmm...eight inches of pure male pleasure." She growled in remembrance, before glancing at the pickle in Rachel's hand and making a sour face. "I can't believe you can eat that."

Rachel grinned and sucked on the dill spear. "I *am* in ecstasy over my pickle. Just the pickle." She looked around to make sure no one listened, before leaning in to add, "And contrary to what you believe, a big penis does not solve all life's problems."

Jac gazed at Rachel as if she'd just blown tea out of her nose.

Rachel shifted under the scrutiny. "Jac, you've rented *Red Shoe Diaries* and *9 ½ Weeks* one too many times. Besides, I'm not sure Brett would appreciate the assessment, pimp woman."

An image of her dream man flashed through Rachel's mind. She saw him above her, on the verge of thrusting inside her aching channel. His perfect ten-inch phallus poised, dripping with dew. Rachel felt herself grow wet.

Brigit laughed and snapped her fingers in front of Rachel's face. "You still with us?"

Right on cue, the telltale warmth of embarrassment spread across her face, until it felt as if her ears would burn off. Rachel sputtered. "I—of course."

Jac leveled her gaze on Rachel, challenge echoing in her voice. "When was the last time you had a good cock? Six months? A year? Never—if you're thinking about Stan, that lame excuse of a fiancé you had a while back."

Rachel flushed anew and shot Jac a pointed look, taking in her friend's fierce expression.

How long has it been since I've had sex? Yikes, two years ago with Stan.

No. Last night, the little voice whispered.

She shook her head and rolled her eyes. I'm losing my mind if I'm considering dream sex as real.

Rachel missed sex.

Maybe the time had come to consider ending her self-imposed abstinence. And she would, just as soon as she got back from the expedition.

"You better enjoy that pickle now, because you're not going to be able to get those, or good cock in that god forsaken jungle." Jac's gaze narrowed into icy slits and her voice lowered to her corporate attorney "this is serious" tone.

Rachel released a heavy breath. Jac had been trying furiously to dissuade her from going on this expedition, since she'd mentioned it to her on the phone earlier this morning.

Brigit took that moment to shove a horoscope in front of Rachel's face. Brigit's mop of red hair hung in arranged disarray. The afternoon sun caught the color, turning it into living flame. Freckles dotted her rosy cheeks and wire-rimmed glasses slipped down her slender nose, giving her a disgruntled funky schoolmarm vibe.

"Jac's right." Brigit poked the paper for emphasis. "The signs are bad. It's all here in black and white. If you go to that jungle you'll be in grave danger."

Rachel shook her head at Brigit's fanaticism for astrology.

Her friend was dressed in a day-glow green skirt, with a matching striped shirt. The color set off her cat-like eyes, making Brigit shine in the ensemble. Anyone else wearing that outfit would have looked like a deformed caterpillar.

"I'm serious," Brigit insisted.

Rachel rolled her eyes and Jac snickered. She knew Jac didn't believe in those kinds of things any more than she did, but Rachel picked up the newspaper clipping and glanced at it before tucking the horoscope into her purse, so that she didn't hurt Brigit's feelings.

"Well?" Brigit glared.

"Thanks, girlfriend. I'll take the fact I'm going to meet a handsome man from a far away land into consideration." Rachel snorted, glancing at Jac, who seemed to be trying desperately not to crack a smile.

"Did you read the bottom?"

Rachel sighed and met Brigit's gaze. "I read the *trouble may come in the form of travel*, but it's not going to stop me from going."

Brigit shook her head and sighed. "Don't say I didn't warn you." She took a big sip of tea, and the loud sucking sound caused people at nearby tables to turn and stare.

Brigit cocked her head and glared at the strangers' faces until they turned away. When her attention came back to the table, she changed the subject. "What hotel are you staying at?"

Rachel giggled behind her napkin at her friend's question. "There are no hotels where I'm going."

Brigit's jaw dropped. "Then where are you going to sleep? A cottage or something?"

"Nope. A tent."

"A tent!" rang out in unison as her friends' voices converged.

"You've never been camping a day in your life!" The color drained from Jac's usual creamy features. "I thought you'd be staying in a village bungalow."

Brigit was aghast. "B-But there are bugs in the jungle and snakes and goodness knows what all."

"You guys." Rachel held up her hand to silence their verbal assault. "I realize that I may not have much experience in the field..."

Jac's brow arched.

"Okay, no field experience." Rachel glanced at Jac and then down at her salad. "But I have waited my whole life for an opportunity like this, and I'm not about to let it pass me by. You know that if I can make a discovery of any kind while I'm there, then Dr. Rumsinger will have to promote me."

"That bastard is just stringing you along," Jac muttered.

Rachel's chin shot up in determination. "Maybe so." She clenched her fork to shore up her defenses. "But if I find something on this expedition and bring it back, then he won't be able to pass me over for a promotion without drawing the attention of the board of directors."

"I don't know, Rachel." Jac shook her head. "It seems like an awfully big risk for the possibility of no returns." She looked to Brigit, who nodded her head in agreement.

Rachel was Jac's pet project. She'd taken Rachel under her wing and had shown her the ropes of socializing and corporate climbing in New York. Jac had even been there to support Rachel's decision to leave Stan.

Rachel decided to take a different tack.

"Brigit, remember when everyone told you that you couldn't break into clothing design without a degree? Who encouraged you to go for it?" Rachel all but begged for an answer.

Her delicate features pinched, Brigit stared for what felt like forever, before nodding begrudgingly. "You did."

Rachel released the breath she'd been holding and turned to Jac's cool gaze. "When you thought you were unprepared to take on the Hiro Corporation as head negotiator in the merger, what did I tell you, Jac?"

"That I'm the ballsiest broad you know and that I could negotiate a boat from a drowning man." Jac ran a trembling hand through her cropped locks. Her hair fell back in place.

"And you did." Rachel paused and looked from Jac's blue eyes to Brigit's green. "You both did. But now it's my turn." Her voice pleaded for understanding.

Jac sighed, a wistful sound that seemed unnatural coming from her. "I'm sorry. You're right. We should be more understanding, but I just don't get why they need you." She took a sip of tea, then patted the side of her mouth with a linen napkin without mussing her blood red lipstick.

With a shrug, Rachel replied. "You know I specialize in ancient languages. Well, the higher-ups figured that although they don't anticipate encountering any natives, other than the hired guides, it wouldn't hurt to have someone along who could communicate if the need arose." She waved her hand dismissively. "They mentioned a lost tribe or some sort of nonsense."

Rachel took a sip of tea and giggled before adding, "I'm sure it pissed Donald off big time to have the board of directors make him take me along, seeing as this is his pet project and all."

Jac snorted.

Brigit's head bobbed in approval. "So you're like 'DATA' or 'C3PO'?" She picked up her sandwich, turning it around and around as if to decide which place was best to bite into.

Rachel laughed. "Leave it to a sci-fi junkie to make that analogy."

"What about safety precautions? What if you get hurt?" Brigit's eyes rounded, concern showing in their green depths. "If I understand you correctly the area you're going into hasn't been well explored."

Rachel nodded. "It is definitely remote, but we'll have several armed guides with us. And the surrounding areas have been mapped and cataloged." She pulled out her guidebook to show them.

Jac picked it from her hands and thumbed through the pages. "This only talks about the animals and plants indigenous to the area." Jac's gaze bored holes in Rachel. "Are you going to carry a gun?"

Rachel nodded. "I've been told it is mandatory, due to unknown factors."

"What unknown factors?" Brigit's brow furrowed. She put her egg salad sandwich back down on the plate.

Rachel couldn't hold back the sarcasm. "If I knew, then they wouldn't be unknown, now would they?"

"Hey don't take that tone with me," Brigit snapped, her voice rising with each word. "Just because you've decided to go gallivanting off into the jungle unprepared."

Rachel blew out a breath in frustration. "I won't be unprepared. We'll have first-aid kits and radios, in case we need to call for help." She didn't bother telling them that radios seemed to pick up weird interference when near the area, which made broadcasting next to impossible. "I'm even going to bring my new GPS cellphone, although I doubt I'll get much of a signal, due to the readings, but you never know."

"What kind of readings?" Jac's voice pinched with pent up tension.

"Strange ones, almost as if the area is a giant vortex. Kind of like the Bermuda Triangle, but on land." Rachel paused, her mind churning with possibilities. "Cool, huh?"

Jac and Brigit frowned. A waiter appeared and refilled their glasses.

Rachel waited for him to leave before she continued. "The readings have been off the charts. It's possible there is an untapped energy source existing at the heart of the rainforest. It would be the discovery of a lifetime if I could locate its source."

"What about the terrain?" Jac asked.

"There are mountains on one side, sheer cliffs on the other, plus a treacherous river that snakes through the area, effectively cutting off the only opening." Rachel grinned as she imagined what the area would look like once she arrived. The photos only gave a minimal idea of the vast expanse. "Oh, and let's not forget the jungle. We really don't know what we'll find until we get there. Heck, it'll take three days just to hike in."

Brigit's face lost all color. "*You're* going to hike?"

"I realize I'm not a tri-athlete like Jac, but I'm not in too bad of shape." Rachel shrugged. "Besides you're one to talk, Brigit. Your idea of a walk is the distance it takes to cross the sidewalk to get to the cab door."

Both women stared at her as if she had a third eye in the center of her forehead. Rachel had meant to lose those last ten pounds months ago, but excuses and Ben and Jerry's got in the way.

The friends ate the rest of their lunch in silence, each left to her own thoughts. Rachel knew she was doing what was right for her. She'd thought by having this lunch that she'd be able to ease her friends' minds and garner their support. Instead, it had backfired. They were now more worried than ever.

Not that she blamed them. If things were reversed, she'd be just as concerned for their welfare.

"If we'd have known we could have gotten you a going away present." Jac grumbled, glancing at Brigit, who nodded.

Expelling a long breath, Rachel pulled out a couple of scraps of paper and a pen from her purse, scrawling while she spoke. "Listen, guys. I want you both to have this number—it's my new cell. Don't worry. I'll be back in three weeks tops. I promise I'll call when I get there. If you like I'll check in every week." She grabbed both their hands, shoving the paper in their palms while giving them a quick squeeze. "So, if you don't hear from me in a week, send in the marines." Rachel laughed at her own joke. "Or you could come, Jac," she continued. "You had that SEAL training from your dad. I wish I'd—"

Jac frowned, her blue eyes clouding with pain from long ago memories.

Crap, why did I say that? Rachel thought. "I'm sorry...you know I didn't mean—"

"Forget about it. I already have." Jac's face resumed its normal flawless mask.

Rachel rubbed her temple, attempting to ease the tension that had taken up residence there. She could just kick herself for being so insensitive. Even after all these years, Jac still had a difficult time dealing with her father's death.

The women were silent as they tucked the papers into their purses. Rachel hated upsetting her friends; they were the closest thing to family she had. If it wasn't for Brigit and Jac, she'd have nothing to return to once the expedition ended.

A cold feeling brushed along Rachel's spine and over her shoulders, as if someone had just walked over her grave. She shivered and rubbed her arms, deciding it was better to keep that little sensation to herself.

Chapter Two

Rachel stared out the tiny plane window. Dirt and bugs were smashed to an even yellow colored paste against the pane.

Through the grunge, snow-capped mountains rose in the distance, their height imposing even from the current altitude. A muddy river wound its way through the jungle alongside a set of sheer cliffs. The rock face was so steep and brittle even the best climbers wouldn't be able to manage scaling its heights.

The turboprop plane swooped over the jungle canopy after circling a dirt strip that passed for a runway. The cleared patch didn't look long enough to accommodate the plane's wingspan, much less the rest of the aircraft. The endless sea of green managed to dwarf everything, including the tiny runway ahead.

Rachel tightened her seatbelt to the point of pain. The small airplane dipped and her stomach lurched and rolled violently. Her mouth watered as the nausea returned. Three hours earlier the turbulence had caused her to lose what little lunch she'd been able to eat.

The plane dropped and within seconds they were level with the treetops. Rachel's heart remained up with the clouds. She started to pray, reciting Hail Marys even though she wasn't Catholic.

Twin engines sputtered and the right wing dipped dangerously toward the primitive strip. The pilot pulled the nose up at the last second and slammed the wheels down. The jarring sensation rattled Rachel's teeth. She probably wouldn't be able to chew solid food again. "Thank God, we made it," she mumbled, understanding now why some people kissed the ground when a flight ended. After this wild ride, she'd seriously consider other modes of transportation in the future.

She glanced out the tiny window as the dirt runway continued to rush past. By her calculations, the team should have already been here for five days. She had traveled the furthest since the Professor had left from a Chicago lecture, which meant she'd arrived last.

The plane halted, sending a cloud of swirling dust in its wake. Jet fumes flooded the main cabin, choking off the stale air.

She coughed, waving her hand in front of her face.

Rachel's fingers trembled as she unfastened her seatbelt and stood on shaky legs. She had to hunch over in the aircraft, which was humorous, considering her five foot two height.

She grabbed her backpack, dragging it up the narrow aisle, and made her way to the open hatch. A crude step had been placed under the door by the pilot for an easy exit, but he had already vanished into the jungle.

Rachel looked down at the step and then back at her massive pack. *How chivalrous of him.*

She stepped off the aircraft into the thick sticky air. The musky scent of earth and flowers surrounded her, permeating every pore, alerting every sense. Her skin tingled. A kind of physical déjà vu spiraled through her, haunting the corners of her mind, like a vision that had become a nightmare. Rachel pushed the dream away, as her body remembered the same strong smells and the dream man with the massive cock.

Her hair instantly frizzed and clung to her neck like a wet blanket. *Man, I thought Central Park in July was bad.*

Searching through her pack, she pulled out a ponytail holder and secured the mop of hair on her head in a half-knot.

Much better.

Rachel shielded her eyes against the sunlight glittering off the silver aircraft. She reached into her shirt pocket and retrieved her sunglasses, slipping them on to fight the midday glare. Lifting her pack onto her shoulder, she hiked a short distance toward what appeared to be base camp. Her boots made soft crunching noises in the loose dirt.

Rachel had walked a few feet when the hair on the nape of her neck stood on end. She swung around, prepared to face an unknown enemy.

No one was there.

Muscles tense, she surveyed the area beyond the aircraft, taking in the dense rainforest. The light didn't seem to penetrate its imposing façade. Her eyes darted along the edge of the vegetation, searching for any sign of movement—a stray monkey or sloth—anything to justify her sudden fear.

Come on city girl, get it together. She shook her head and continued on.

* * * * *

Eros watched the woman exit the silver plane, his eyes lingering on the rounded curves of her hips and voluptuous breasts that begged for his touch. Would her nipples be like the ripe berries growing on the vines, red, tempting and oh so sweet?

The prediction had been correct — the woman from the seer's vision had finally arrived. He'd staked out the encampment for five days, but hadn't spotted any females.

Until now.

He released the breath he'd been holding. His large frame rippled with acute awareness. The woman seemed small, unusually so, but still...there was something about her that stirred him.

Her brown curly hair hung low across the womanly flair of her hips. He wondered what it would feel like to have that hair wrapped around his fist while he buried himself deep inside her.

Eros followed her movements, insatiable hunger searing through him. Her nimble fingers grasped the mass of curls, tying them quickly, exposing more of her ripe heart-shaped bottom to his seeking eyes. Would her feminine musk surround him tauntingly, enveloping his senses until his lust was uncontrollable?

His mouth went dry and his cock bucked beneath his loincloth, hardening instantly. Breathing became difficult. The need to possess, claim, conquer, overwhelmed him. Ariel, the seer, hadn't mentioned these turbulent emotions when she told him about her vision.

Confusion swamped him.

The woman stopped midway and looked in his direction. Her full lips pursed and her pale complexion glowed against the sunlight as she searched the jungle.

She sensed his presence.

Eros smiled. He liked the fact she felt him, knew he watched her from the shadows. He stepped back, even though she wouldn't be able to spot him in his hiding place amongst the trees.

He would take no chances when it came to this woman. She was too important to his people.

To him.

* * * * *

Men bustled from tent to tent. Temporary housing had been set up, covered wagon style, with the center being the main gathering area. Charred remnants from a fire dotted the middle like a wagon wheel. All flaps opened in, which seemed strange, but then again Rachel didn't know much about camping, and this *was* the jungle.

Rachel reached the tent where most of the activity seemed to be occurring. She stopped outside the open flap, trying to shore up her courage to face Dr. Donald Rumsinger, or Professor as he liked to be called. Her boss, her nemesis, the biggest pain in the ass she'd ever had the displeasure of meeting. He'd been jealous of her popularity at the museum since day one. Rachel had never considered herself a threat, but to Dr. Rumsinger she was. He remained convinced that despite her lack of seniority, when an upper level position opened, she would get it. Rachel shook her head and rolled her eyes. *As if...*She'd be happy with the promotion Donald dangled over her head at present.

Like it was yesterday, she remembered the day she'd learned what a truly vile human being he was. Donald had requested she meet him at his office to discuss a new find. When she'd arrived there had been a note taped to the door, saying he'd be right back and could she please retrieve the broom from the janitor's closet and clean up the mess on the floor.

He'd shattered a glass.

She'd been aggravated that he considered her nothing more than a glorified cleanup girl, but decided it wasn't worth arguing. So like a sap, Rachel went to the closet door and pulled it open…

Catching the Professor in the act of having sex with another man, Dr. Todd.

Rachel had never suspected Dr. Todd's homosexuality. Todd had taken her under his wing on her first day of work. They would usually have lunch together and had discussed problems the museum faced with future funding. On occasion they'd chatted about their personal lives or lack thereof.

She'd actually had a sort of schoolgirl crush on him, when she'd first hired on. She hadn't done a good job of hiding that from him or anyone else. He was gorgeous and all the women at the museum wanted him.

After she'd discovered him in the closet with Donald, her dear friend Dr. Todd had been unable to look her in the eye.

She grimaced.

When she'd opened the closet door, the Professor had leered at her, his evil eyes glittering with amusement — while Dr. Todd looked mortified, scrambling to cover his impressive privates.

Donald did everything for his own entertainment and didn't care who he hurt in the process.

The mean-spirited bastard.

She didn't give one flip if Dr. Todd was gay. She missed his friendship.

Rachel blew out a breath. It was now or never. She pulled back the flaps and entered the canvas tent. Dr. Donald Rumsinger stood next to the satellite tracking equipment, his hands full of cables.

Black wires were strung out over the silver top as Donald studied topographical images. His orange-red hair lay slicked back with a goopy gel, and thick black glasses, suspended on a bulbous nose, enlarged his mud brown eyes to inhuman proportions. A long walrus tusk shaped mustache hung low, covering his jowls. His potbelly strained the buttons of his soiled shirt. The Professor's bushy brows were furrowed and his face creased with what looked like worry.

As if realizing someone was staring, he looked up. His expression changed instantly to one of disgust. "Dr. Evans, how good of you to *finally* join us." His voice was contemptuous as a slight smile split his ruddy face.

Rachel swallowed her automatic retort, *asshole.*

Play nice, Rachel.

She wished she had the nerve to wipe that smug smile right off his rotund face. But even several thousand miles away from home, he was still her boss.

Rachel wouldn't let the "talking walrus" get to her. She was too close to obtaining her dream promotion to let petty differences get in the way.

She managed a smile. "Hello Professor. How nice to *see* you again." She didn't have to add *with your clothes on* for him to get the picture.

The man's face colored at the emphasis.

She tried not to gag as she pictured Donald's flaccid red prick dripping with semen as he pulled it out of Dr. Todd's ass. Donald hadn't even had sense enough to use a condom.

He cleared his throat. "Yes, well…" Donald expelled a frustrated breath. "We'll get started tomorrow morning at the crack of dawn. I just need to fix some of the equipment damaged last night."

She looked around the rest of the tent at the disarray. "What happened?"

"Seems someone decided to try to sabotage our expedition by slicing through the back of the tent and cutting random wires. But," he waved his meaty hand dismissively, "don't worry, they didn't succeed."

"But who — what?"

"One of the natives, most likely. Superstitious bastards. I've told them if anymore *accidents* occur I'll dock their pay." He smiled, obviously pleased with the power he held over the poor locals' heads.

Rachel planted her hands on her hips and her voice cracked. "What accidents?"

"One of the guides died down by the stream." He shrugged his heavy shoulders. "No great loss."

Rachel's face flushed and she brought her palm to her forehead, rubbing it back and forth, trying to cool the area, as she considered the situation. "How?"

"Some sort of jungle creature. Probably anaconda or perhaps a black caiman." Donald paused, pulling on his whiskers. "I suppose it could have been a cat." He laughed. "Just one of the many risks that comes with the job. You don't want to leave, do you?"

The hopeful note in his voice made Rachel's stomach flip. Someone had died, and the Professor made it sound like he'd simply rid himself of excess baggage.

Asshole.

Rachel took a ragged breath. Her fingers trembled as she fought back the same cold fear she'd felt yesterday. "I didn't think there were large cats in the area."

"I had to tell them something to calm the group down. We can't have the guides panicking, now can we? They must be willing to enter the rainforest."

The man was truly a heartless bastard. If he weren't in charge of the expedition, she'd tell him exactly where he could stick his attitude.

But she couldn't and wouldn't, because like the poor locals, he could have her bounced out of here in a heartbeat. Rachel found someone to point out where her tent was located and then phoned Jac, only to get her answering machine. The woman was never home. Rachel left a message letting her know that the flight arrived more or less on time and everything appeared to be on schedule. She hung up after saying she'd call her in a week, purposely omitting the fact that the expedition had already encountered sabotage.

* * * * *

Night fell quickly in the jungle. The air in the tent grew smothering as Rachel unpacked only essentials. The cot, on the other hand, was actually quite comfortable once she put the sleeping bag down and mosquito netting up.

She peeked out the door. A fire blazed in the center of the group of tents. Some of the men gathered away from the flames, sitting in a circle and swapping what appeared to be fishing stories.

Rachel tied the flap of the tent up in hopes of catching a breeze, any kind of relief from the stifling conditions. She walked into the clearing, near the log stumps positioned around the fire.

She took a seat on one of the logs, furthest from the flames. It was unbearably hot, the air so thick that it hung in low, shadowy clouds just above the treetops, pressing down on the creatures below in a smothering embrace. A cacophony of insects swirled in the night sky, their buzzing surprisingly soothing.

Winged creatures, probably bats, dove close to the fire, pulling up at the last minute in amazing aerial acrobatic feats. Monkeys squealed, their haunting cries so human-like she found it disconcerting.

In the distance she could just barely make out the sound of rushing water through the wall of trees. A stream definitely ran nearby, probably the one the Professor had mentioned. Rachel squinted, trying to pierce the darkness. She couldn't see any sign of the stream or the three-quarter moon's reflection on anything resembling the tempting liquid.

A cool dip in running water would feel like heaven right about now. Anything to get the sweat off her body. But it was dangerous to go near the stream. Predators came out to hunt, and the most vulnerable prey was found near water.

Perspiration dripped between her breasts, saturating the bottom of her bra. Loose tendrils of hair clung to her temples. The back of her shirt was soaked down the center, and sticking to her like a second skin.

She walked back to her tent and pulled out the zoological guidebook from the case containing her work papers. It had arrived yesterday with Donald's supply shipment and had been placed inside her tent. As she flipped through the pages in the glow of the kerosene lantern, she read up on what little was known about the local predators.

The waters in this area weren't supposed to be home to piranha. Only the occasional anaconda and crocodile lived in these parts, but were mainly found deeper in the jungle. According to the book, the animals had been pushed further in due to mans' encroachment.

An anaconda would make a meal out of her in seconds, probably before she could even scream. Fortunately, the snakes didn't eat every day because of their slow metabolism. It was lucky for her that the efficient predators tended to avoid running water, preferring instead to use calm pools to drown their victims.

Lovely image.

Sweat dripped from her chin onto her book. She slammed it closed, her decision made. She'd rather take on an anaconda than turn into a puddle. She dropped the book on the cot and grabbed a towel from her pack, along with a change of clothes. Her hand dug deep trying to arrange the items into some semblance of neatness. Satisfied, Rachel reached for the zoological guide to return it to her work case. She was pushing papers aside when her hand struck something hard. Rachel pulled the item from the case. A semi-automatic Glock dangled from her fingertips with a note taped to it from Jac.

You didn't think I'd let you go down there without taking one of my little friends with you, did you? Love, Jac.

Rachel glanced over at her cot. A pistol had been placed in her tent by one of the workers. Her lips twisted into a smile as she reread Jac's note. She laughed, then tucked the present into the bottom of her tote for safekeeping. It was far too visible in her work case. Anyone could find it. Rachel didn't even question how Jac had managed to get it in there. Some things were best left unknown. She picked up the guide-supplied pistol, taking a few minutes to get used to its unusual weight in her hand. She didn't like guns, never had.

She gathered a flashlight and tucked all the items into her safari shirt pockets. When she looked out of the tent, her eyes were drawn to a young native nearby. With a wave of her hand, she signaled for him to come over.

Shy brown eyes looked warily at her beneath long black lashes. His face was a flawless brown coffee color. She decided to speak to the young man in his local dialect, as opposed to English. His face brightened instantly and dimples appeared on his cheeks.

She asked where the path to the water was located. He shook his head and looked around, his eyes darting nervously from shadow to shadow. Rachel reassured him that he wouldn't get into trouble if he just pointed her in the right direction.

He hesitated.

Rachel gave him an encouraging look and he acquiesced. She took out a few dollars and pressed them in his small hand. He flashed her a quick smile and then bolted. Rachel watched his retreating form until he disappeared out of sight, before turning to gaze into the darkness. She shivered, despite the heat, her gaze searching the inky blackness for any cause of her unease. She shook off the unwanted feeling.

* * * * *

From the darkness, sharp eyes watched the woman leave her tent. She made a right and headed down the trail in the direction of the water. Eros smiled.

Come to me, my Queen.

Chapter Three

Rachel made her way, flashlight in hand, down a trail she hadn't seen earlier in the day. Ferns were thick around her ankles and vines hung haphazardly across the path. The sound of crashing water grew louder, swallowing up all trace of the camp behind her. She could almost feel the refreshing spray upon her heated skin.

Several minutes passed, the trail widened a bit and the water roared. Orchids clung to the sides of trees like babes to teats, their blooms sweetening the air. Rachel pushed a vine out of the way and stepped into a tiny clearing. A waterfall tumbled from a small outcropping of rocks, plunging into a churning pool. Ten feet further the frothy water turned placid, the current gentle, as it meandered out of sight. *Anaconda territory.*

The swirling liquid looked amazingly black, even with the reflection of the three- quarter moon shining upon its surface, casting an ethereal glow. She glanced up. Never in all the years of living in New York had Rachel ever seen a sky as wondrous as this star-spattered blanket of ebony.

A breeze caught spray from the waterfall, gently misting her face. She closed her eyes, enjoying the sudden refreshment. Leaves crunched nearby.

Rachel's eyes flew open and she whirled around, flashlight in hand, frantically trying to catch any sign of movement. Which was nearly impossible with her fingers trembling like she'd polished off five pots of coffee. It looked more like she tried to hail aliens, than spot the culprit.

Her beam passed quickly over a set of glowing red eyes.

She jerked the light back, but in the second it took the glowing orbs were gone. Her brows furrowed and she shook her head. The specks had been too large to be anything other than her imagination. Nonetheless, she scrutinized the area again, shining the beam on the tree branches and the jungle floor —

Nothing.

Anacondas do not have big round eyes. It must have been a trick of the light.

She pictured Dr. Rumsinger's bespectacled orbs and laughed. She was pretty sure no one would feel more repulsed by her nakedness than Donald, if he were lurking in the shadows. It would serve him right to be disgusted considering the stunts he'd pulled on her.

Rachel set the light down and began to undress. The pistol fell out of her pocket with a muted clunk.

Smooth move, Rachel. If you shoot yourself in the foot you'll never be able to go back to the museum and face your co-workers. There's nothing here, so relax.

She reached down and scooted the weapon away from the water's edge, but still within easy reach if she needed to get to it. Rachel expelled a breath she hadn't known she'd been holding, and pulled her clinging shirt from her body. It made a disgusting, sucking noise. Rachel cringed and decided unless she wore rubber, clothes should never make those kinds of sounds. She removed her bra and her nipples sprang to life, beading instantly in the hot humid air. She placed her clothes next to the gun.

Rachel smiled and stretched her arms slowly, luxuriously above her head. "Ah...that's better."

As she reached down to untie her hiking boots, the hair at her nape rose. She grabbed the flashlight and swung it around wildly, but once again the beam landed on nothing. Not even a monkey lurked near the edge of the water. She blew out a steadying breath.

Definitely a city girl.

Shrugging, she set the light back down and untied her laces, toeing off the boots. She worked the buttons on her pants until they were loose enough to slide over her hips. Rachel stood next to the pool in her lace underwear, listening.

Insects had stopped singing and the jungle had fallen still. Her heart pounded as her fight or flight response kicked in.

Something watched her from the jungle.

Please don't let it be a predator.

She waited for a several minutes, heart slamming in her chest, until the feeling of being watched went away. Rachel sent a small prayer of thanks up to the heavens, then shucked off her underwear and made a shallow dive into the water. Slicing through the churning liquid, she surfaced several yards from the shore. The water pooled just deep enough to reach her full breasts. She hoped against hope that if anything was out there, whatever *it* was couldn't swim.

Nothing moved.

She looked all around, waiting. She dunked her head under the water again to pull her hair from her face.

When she broke the surface the flashlight was off.

A chill raced up her spine.

Snakes don't turn lights off. Only men.

Expressing more bravado than she actually felt, she shouted, "Show yourself."

Her eyes frantically darted around the thick canopy. She caught no sign of movement. Gradually, her vision adjusted to the dark. Rachel could make out monkeys skulking along branches and bats flying in the night sky.

A swift movement caught her eye. Something large loomed about twenty yards away in the darkness. Its massive frame moved effortlessly and silently amongst the trees.

She tried to recall the guidebook's entry on animals. There wasn't any documented creature of that size inhabiting the area.

"Professor, is that you?" she asked, realizing as she spoke there was no way Donald could have produced that size shadow.

No answer.

"Come on, stop fooling around. This isn't funny anymore." Her voice quivered.

Suddenly the threatening feeling shifted, morphed into something...familiar, which wasn't possible, was it? Rachel felt flushed, as if the creature's eyes were skimming over her body like licking flames, roaming, exploring, and cataloging every square inch of her exposed flesh. Mapping her hidden areas for later exploration.

Rachel had the urge to dip down in the water, effectively covering herself from its seeking gaze. Her little-used body had other ideas, and her nipples pebbled in response, engorging with blood until they ached.

A little voice in her head asked. *What would Jac do?*

Letting out a haggard breath, she took a tentative step toward shore, exposing her breasts fully. Her skin prickled as the water cascaded down the valley between her voluptuous globes, like a thousand tiny licking caresses.

Rachel thought she heard a groan, but the roar of the water muffled all sound. She paused, listening, trying to decide just how far she was willing to show herself. After all, she wasn't sure precisely what or whom she dealt with here.

A smile curved her full lips as she pictured exactly what her friend Jac would do in this situation. Rachel reached up slowly with her hands and placed her fingers over the tips of her breasts and tugged gently, fondling the peaks.

A strangled sound came from the darkest part of the jungle. Empowered, she pulled at her nipples, her movements deliberate and sensual, circling them until they marbled. The dusky tips quivered and throbbed with need.

It's probably one of the guides, hiding by the trees. Rachel decided to give him a good show, a sort of twisted punishment for spying on her.

She took another step and the water level dropped to mid-thigh, exposing her pussy. Droplets of water clung to the thick nest of sable hair covering her clit. Rachel reluctantly pulled one hand from her nipple and ran her fingertips over the soft, curving flesh of her waist, straight for the sensitive nub buried beneath her mound. With seduction in mind, she slid her finger over her wet folds and felt her body flush anew with its natural juices.

Rachel moaned.

Her breathing hitched. Suddenly she wasn't just teasing some stranger in the dark. Her body wanted this, needed this, longed for this and knowing someone out there watched only made it more erotic.

She picked up the rhythm as her body tightened in readiness, her orgasm drawing nearer.

Rachel took a couple more steps and reached the shore. Her wobbly legs refused to go further. She dropped down on the grassy bank, falling over onto her back, now cushioned by the lush vegetation. One hand pulled at her nipples while the other, slick with pussy juice, continued to work its magic pleasuring her.

She was hot, needy, and ready.

Rachel, you're in a jungle where the nearest worthy candidate for a good fuck is over a thousand miles away, was her last coherent thought before she succumbed to pure sensation.

Her hips undulated and the muscles in her abdomen bunched as the familiar pleasure-pain started. Blood rushed through her head, deafening the sounds around her, until they faded to a distant hum.

Faster and faster she stroked her clit as if possessed, wrapped in a world of carnal need. Her legs shook. The tension in her abdomen pulled taut, teetering on the precipice of that elusive peak, ready to plummet to the awaiting bliss.

A loud moan tore from Rachel's throat as she came hard. The orgasm slammed into her, washing over her in wave after wave of hot slicing pleasure. Warmth spread through her and out to her limbs, leaving everything tingling. She continued her movements, milking her body, until there was nothing left but afterglow.

* * * * *

Eros couldn't tear his eyes from the woman. Every fiber of his being screamed out to her, demanding her attention. His heated gaze followed her pale hands as they moved over her full breasts, squeezing at the nipples until they protruded like ripe red berries. He had managed to turn off the light and grab her gun before she'd been able to spot him.

Her creamy skin glowed in the darkness, smooth and satiny, flushed and glistening, from the dip in the pool. He watched as she slid her fingers between her rounded thighs and began strumming the damp petals of her womanhood.

Moonlight reflected off the juices seeping from her body, the fragrance as rare as the gold orchid. His cock stiffened like a ramrod. Eros moaned in discomfort. He removed the pistol she'd dropped earlier from his waistband, letting it fall to the weeds. The weapon had no place near his woman.

Her body rippled, slinking with each tantalizing feminine vibration.

She was killing him.

He shook as he tried to maintain the energy surge he'd sent out to ward off the nearby predators so that she'd be protected in the water. Her wild scent called out, beckoning him to mount her, mate with her, possess her.

Eros wrapped his hand around his throbbing cock, his fingers subconsciously mirroring her movements, pumping furiously. The scene before him was too much.

She was too much.

He had to force himself to stay in the shadows, when everything inside told him to go to her, plunge inside, fuck her mindless. He held his breath, stroking himself harder and faster. Like he wanted to be thrusting inside the woman. He imagined her hot sheath closing around his cock, gripping.

She continued with her frantic undulations, her fingers slick from her probing. Rounded hips pumped against her hand as she reached her peak. She moaned in release at the same time he spilled his seed.

Eros groaned. His body jerked violently, lean muscles bunching in taut lines as he ejaculated. Semen jettisoned out over his hand and onto the ferns below, leaving him hot and sticky.

He couldn't seem to catch his breath. His lungs heaved with the effort and his vision blurred. He shuddered as his cock began to lose some of its hardness. Still he gripped himself, wishing the woman held him instead, refusing to let go of the lingering sensation.

The woman was a sorceress.

Not since he was a young man had he been so careless, so out of control. Eros fisted his hands in frustration. He didn't like the fact that this woman already had a firm hold on him. The seer had withheld that information. After a couple of agonizing gasps, he slowed his breathing.

Eros watched her breasts rise and fall, their fullness jiggling with each breath. The movement held him spellbound. He longed to lap at the pale globes, swirl his tongue around the rosy peaks until her arousal consumed her once again. Just thinking about it had him growing hard once again.

He vowed the next time she cried out in pleasure, it would be his name forming on her lips.

He'd make sure of it.

Eros turned away from the woman, unable to gaze upon her naked form any longer. His massive body trembled as he fought the urge to seize.

Unconcerned with being heard, he made his way through the jungle, snapping limbs and vines along his route with his powerful hands. He walked a few yards further, then wailed, letting out a warrior's battle cry. The action released all remaining pent up tension from his body.

Vision be damned, he wasn't waiting any longer.

* * * * *

Rachel's breathing remained choppy as she gradually floated back to reality. She slowed her movements down to a few quick strokes, the kind you'd give a cat.

She laughed and brought her arms up and covered her eyes, grasping her elbows and inhaling deeply. The musky smell of sex on her fingers swamped her, the unmistakable odor wafted around mingling with the flowers, permeating the area.

She sighed, contented.

Something crashed near the edge of the trees. Rachel leapt up, her hands flying immediately to protect her exposed flesh. She reached around in the grass, found the light and flicked it on, but its beam was unable to penetrate more than a few feet.

The darkness pressed in around her, surrounding, encircling and immovable. She tossed the light down and grabbed her clothes, throwing the items on in haste.

A tormented cry bellowed out, echoing throughout the jungle. Nothing that she'd ever heard before sounded like that. Birds took flight, squawking in panic. Monkeys scattered and nocturnal creatures scurried for places to hide.

Rachel snatched the flashlight and ran up the trail, tearing at the vines in her way. She felt eyes boring into her back. *What have I done?*

Plants and twigs crashed behind her, closer and closer. Her hair snagged on something for a second, before gaining release. She could have sworn large fingers had given her a quick stroke.

Yeah, girl, and Tarzan is going to sweep down from the trees, snatch you up into his muscled arms and carry you off to his hut.

Rachel broke from the jungle in a full sprint. Men were hollering and running from tent to tent with guns in their hands, their eyes bulging, wild with fear. Her arms immediately went in the air as several rifles swung around and pointed in her direction. She slowed but didn't stop. Another strangled cry permeated the night.

And then it hit her — she'd forgotten her pistol.

She wasn't going back for it now. Rachel didn't stop running until she reached the entrance of her tent. She dove through the opening, pulling the flap closed behind her. She zipped the door and tied all the straps. Her lungs labored for breath, choppy gulps were all she could manage after the sprint.

Her heart pounded out a rapid tattoo as she undressed. Her fingers shook from excess adrenaline as she buttoned her over-sized pajama top and slipped into her cot. She placed the mosquito netting around her and stared blindly at the ceiling.

She'd been hunted tonight and had barely escaped capture.

The question was, by what?

* * * * *

Eros looked over his shoulder and saw the woman bolt. Instinct kicked in and he ran after her, a predator hunting its prey.

He reined in his desire, tightly leashing it. He could easily overtake her, but he chose to wait. The camp was already in an uproar due to his foolishness. In the end, she'd come to him. This group would enter the jungle tomorrow. Then they'd be in his territory.

She'd be his…soon.

He reached out a second before she broke from the trees and allowed his fingers to brush against the wet hair clinging to her back. It was soft, like he knew it would be.

Perhaps he'd pay her a visit.

Yes—tonight once all had calmed. He'd taste what he'd been denied moments ago. In the end, her body would be his.

* * * * *

The camp settled down after a couple of watchful hours. Eros made his way through the jungle, following the tree line to the backside of the tents. Hers was easy enough to pick out, since he'd memorized the layout earlier in the week.

He'd gathered the herbs needed to ensure she would be aware of his presence, but not fully awake. The mixture grew pungent as he ground the herbs together into a fine powder, adding his natural energy to the mix. He was immune to the plants effects, as were his fellow Atlanteans.

All he had to do was make it to her tent and slip inside before the guides guarding the campsite noticed. He moved silently, his stealth legendary amongst his people.

He reached the back of her tent. No one saw him slip the razor sharp blade from its sheath and slice through the canvas. *Just as easy the second time, as it was the first.* In moments the opening expanded, big enough for him to slip his large frame inside.

The woman slept beneath netting, protecting her delicate skin from damaging pests. Her breathing flowed deep and steady. In her sleep she made little mewling sounds and her limbs twitched as she dreamt. Eros smiled.

He approached her inert form and knelt down beside the cot. With trembling fingers, he carefully separated the netting to gain access to her alabaster face.

She was beautiful up close, small and compact, yet full and curvy in all the right places. The light from the campfire brightened the inside of the tent, casting dancing shadows across her pale features.

She smelled of rain and earth, flowers and spice. Eros lifted a finger to brush an escaping brown tendril from her forehead, the texture reminiscent of the finest silk. She stirred, her rosy lips puckering as if accepting a lover's kiss.

Need once again slammed into him, along with rage the likes of which he'd never experienced. From this day forth she'd have no other lovers. Calming his turbulent emotions, he reached into his pouch and pulled out the white concoction. Carefully, he took some of the powder into his palm and gently blew the contents across her face.

She inhaled deeply. Her nose twitched and she let out a delicate sneeze. Her eyes fluttered open and locked on his. They widened instantly. Her pupils dilated from exposure to the waking sleep drug. She stared at him as if she recognized him, which was impossible. Eros sensed no fear, only curiosity.

"Shh...you're dreaming," he whispered. Her brows furrowed slightly. "My name is Eros. You won't remember that by tomorrow, but it's important that you know it now, for I want to hear it as you cry out when you come for me." She continued her perusal, her eyes reflecting a myriad of questions, before a slow seductive smile formed on her lips. Apparently the thought of having him pleasure her in her dreams wasn't unappealing.

The muscles in his chest constricted and his heart did a little flip-flop.

Eros dismissed the sensation as quickly as it had arrived. He reached down to the front of her sleep clothing to unbutton her top. His eyes stayed on her face, looking for any sign of fear or disapproval. He would not force his woman tonight.

He simply couldn't resist the urge to touch her softness, feel her wetness, and hear her soft cries when she came for him.

When the fabric opened and fell away from her body, he tore his eyes from her face. Even with the faint lighting, he could still make out her creamy features. His breath stole from his lungs. Her breasts were large, like he preferred.

He traced his callused finger along her jaw, down her neck, over her collarbone, until he reached the full globes. Goose flesh rose up on her body and her eyes narrowed to tiny desire-filled slits. His fingertip circled one nipple, teasing, drawing it out until it puckered into a tightly aroused peak. Eros withdrew his finger, replacing it with his hungry mouth.

She moaned as his lips latched on to the beaded areola, the sound so exquisite that for a moment he closed his eyes in ecstasy. His tongue flicked over the succulent flesh, making the tight berry marble in response. He reached up with his free hand and pinched her other nipple gently between his finger and thumb, the rough pad stimulating her enough for her to release another soft moan.

Eros sucked in once more, then ripped himself away from her breasts. He wanted more, needed more. He would accept nothing less than her complete surrender. He closed his eyes, trying to gather strength enough to be able to stop when the time came.

"Are you ready for me?" he asked, unable to hide the huskiness in his voice.

She tried to move, but was unable. He smiled at her, then slid down until he rested his arms on her thighs. He leaned forward a few inches above the scrap of material covering the crisp curls of her mound and inhaled. He filled his lungs deeply. She smelled of the sweetest flower, the richest delicacy, her arousal thick and musky in the still night air. It was his turn to bite back a groan.

"You want me little one?" Eros breathed in once more, cataloging her scent within his body, taking her essence into his soul, so that if she escaped he'd be able to find her anywhere.

"Yes," she murmured, her voice thick from the drug.

He had the urge to mark her as his own. Claim her for all time. His hard cock jumped within its confines, demanding the freedom to seek her warm channel.

Not until after the ceremony. The seer's warning echoed in his mind.

Eros ran a lone finger along the edge of her lace panties, then pulled out his knife, lifted the seam and sliced them off. He brought the material to his nose, inhaling again, then quickly tucked the ruined panties into his loincloth. His finger delved among her slick folds and into her wet slit, gently separating the petals that hid her fiery pearl.

Rachel mewled.

Her juices gushed over his hand. He brought the finger to his mouth and slipped it inside, tasting her for the first time. His mouth exploded in sensation, savoring, relishing, and filing her unique flavor for future reference.

Exotic like forbidden fruit, she was truly a gift from the goddess.

He pulled the finger from his mouth, maneuvering his bulk to the end of the cot, before slipping both hands onto her rounded thighs, carefully separating them enough until he could press his wide shoulders between them. Her breathing came out ragged, on edge with anticipation.

Eros pulled her down until her bottom hit the lip of the cot. She was exposed and dripping, her wet pussy longing for what he would give her.

She murmured, seemingly unable to form coherent words.

He slipped a finger inside her velvet sheath. "You like this, don't you little one?"

A long, needy moan pushed past her lips. Eros worked his finger in and out of her. The muscles of her hungry cunt gripped him, beckoning him, pulling him back inside. He added another finger.

She was tight, very tight. She would need much preparation before she'd be able to accommodate his massive cock. He removed his fingers from her moist folds. He needed more. Eros lowered his head between her legs and stuck out his six-inch tongue, stiffening it in preparation for entry. His eyes met hers a second before he plunged inside her passage.

She gasped and whimpered. Her body rippled. He fucked her with his tongue, lapping at her folds in between each thrust, branding her. His thumb found her clit. He applied pressure to the hidden treasure with each circling pass.

She cried out softly, her heated flesh singing beneath his masterful touch. Her body began to tremble and quake, riding on the razor's edge of desire. He continued to plunder for a few minutes more, lapping up her juices.

Eros paused, his muscles quivering. He met her eyes and waited for the word he needed to hear her utter.

She gasped, making keening noises deep in her throat, trying to tilt her pussy to his face. "Eros, please…"

There it was—his name. He dove back between her legs, twisting and spiraling his tongue, his mouth frenzied, drunk with the smell of her impending release.

Giving one last shudder, Rachel came hard in his mouth, her body rippling with aftershocks.

Eros fed deep from her endless well.

He licked her flowing juices, trying to catch every last drop with his tongue. Intoxicated by her taste, he savored her wetness, praying that the memory would last until he could feast upon her once again.

Mindlessly, he stroked the soft down between her legs, petting it for a job well done. His eyes followed her pebble-like nipples moving up and down, until her breathing slowed. The rise and fall of her chest mesmerized, lulling him with its calming rhythm.

His chin was wet from her release. Eros wiped it with the back of his hand and onto his loincloth. His cock grew so hard, he thought it would burst before he'd get a chance to fill her. How he'd last until after the ceremony, he knew not.

"Sleep little one."

The creatures of the jungle were starting to stir. In a few hours it would be dawn. With great effort, he rose up, quickly buttoning her shirt and moving her back onto the cot.

Her eyes were drowsy from being sated. He placed a slow burning kiss on her mouth. His teeth nipped at her lower lip, until she allowed him full access, until she surrendered.

Eros's heart leapt in triumph.

He plunged into her deep recesses, tasting the honeyed nectar within. In a dance as old as time itself, her tongue tangoed with his, turning, dipping and rotating, voracious in its demands for a deeper connection.

Reluctantly he pulled away from her, fighting the primal urges coursing through his body. He replaced the netting around her cot and slipped out the same way he'd come. *See you tomorrow, my Queen.*

Chapter Four

Dawn's pink tentacles stretched across the vast blue sky. Animals scurried in the underbrush, crunching leaves and small ferns beneath their clawed feet. Filling the air with a dissonant symphony, macaws and parrots sang out, each vying to outdo the other.

Rachel rubbed her bloodshot eyes, pretty sure someone had dumped a pound of sand in them sometime during the night. Her head pounded like a jackhammer, threatening to roll off her shoulders. Muscles ached as if she hadn't slept a wink. The strange cry had echoed in her mind, refusing to let her drift off until the hour drew late.

To make matters worse she'd had the most erotic dream of her life, similar to the ones she'd had back in New York. Yet this one was different because last night she'd finally seen her dream man's face.

The beauty of his features made him even more godlike than before. The dream had felt so *real*, sizzling flesh upon flesh. And that tongue, mmm. Just the thought sent a jolt of electricity slicing through her.

No more masturbating until I return to New York.

She shook her head, trying to clear the fogginess that had taken up residence. The tent smelled like a spice rack had been emptied in it. Awareness tingled at the back of her mind.

Rachel had detected the same odor last night in her dream. Rising, she slipped her pajama top over her head.

As she folded the cotton she noticed the buttons were off by one.

Rachel shrugged. She hadn't seen it last night, but it wouldn't be the first time she'd buttoned her sleep shirt the wrong way. Besides, she'd been all thumbs because of her scare down by the water.

Her black lace underwear was missing. Had she gotten so caught up in the dream that she'd slipped them off during the night? If so, then where could she have put them? She'd heard of wet dreams, but this was ridiculous.

She searched through the crumpled material in her pack, confused and slightly embarrassed by her lack of control. Rachel donned clean clothes and pulled her hair back, securing the mop under a New York Yankees baseball cap.

She rolled her sleeping bag and folded all her things into her pack, including the mosquito netting. She was set.

Pulling a rose colored lipstick out of one of the pockets, she applied it without the use of a mirror. *No sense roughing it too much.*

She was about to untie the flaps on the door when a flash of sunlight out of the corner of her eye caught her attention. She walked to the back wall of her tent, and saw that a thin line of light shown through. Her brows furrowed as she examined the fabric. The slice was clean, as if it had been cut with a very sharp instrument.

Just like the back of the equipment tent.

Fear gripped her in a tight fist, sending the air rushing from her lungs. Rachel ran her hands along the rough edges of the three-foot opening. Her heart began to pound frantically, stampeding in her chest until she thought it might burst. With trembling fingers she pulled the area apart. It opened to the jungle.

She looked into the heavy underbrush. Her eyes scanned the thick growth, searching for anything that could put an end to her growing panic. Nothing.

He wasn't a dream, screamed in her mind with increasing volume.

She dropped the flap and turned to the entrance of her tent. She unzipped the door and exited quickly. Her hands refused to stop shaking.

People bustled around the fire. The wet jungle air surrounded her, enticing, beckoning, and thankfully calming her rising anxiety. She had to get a grip.

Last night she'd let a stranger caress her, kiss her, and make love to her with his tongue. Was it the same man who had watched her at the stream? Had she issued an unspoken invitation when she'd put on the erotic show? It had seemed so harmless at the time.

She shook her head in denial. Surely not. The jungle was already making her crazy. Making her see and do things she wouldn't normally do in her everyday life. Or at least making her think she had done them. Rachel rubbed her forehead.

Was it possible to get jungle fever in a day? Rachel didn't think so, and besides jungle fever didn't explain her missing underwear.

The smell of coffee brewing and bacon cooking permeated her senses, bringing her back from her reverie. Her stomach growled. There wasn't much she could do about the dream man at this point. If he was real, he was probably long gone by now. She hoped.

Rachel walked to the table where breakfast had been laid out. She grabbed a slice of bacon and popped it into her mouth, eating it while she took in the rest of the offerings.

She spied a corn muffin, reached for it and took a big bite. It crumpled in her mouth, the sweet taste blending deliciously with the saltiness of the bacon. She found a mug and poured herself a cup of the black java and took a sip, testing the temperature. The bitter liquid washed the muffin down.

"Ah, Starbucks eat your heart out." She laughed at her own joke. It was amazing how being out in the middle of nowhere changed your perception of what tasted good.

And changed your perception of reality.

Professor Donald exited a tent with his khakis on. A young native man peered out through the flaps behind him, shoulders slumped, a hollow look upon his face. The Professor shoved some money into the man's outstretched hand, his lip curled into a sneer. The native raced from the tent and straight into the jungle without looking back.

Rachel glared at the "talking walrus" and shook her head in disgust. The man was a parasite. The Professor just smiled, spreading his arms wide and patting his stomach as if nothing was amiss.

She took her coffee and walked to the fire. Already the jungle's temperature spiked near eighty and it wasn't even six yet. Rachel sipped her coffee, watching the rest of the camp come to life.

Men started moving belongings to the center circle and taking down the tents. Equipment was packed in heavy-duty crates and loaded, some into the plane and others onto strong native backs. Their busy movements reminded Rachel of an ant farm, coordinated, precise, and organized.

"You have time to go down to the stream if you want, Dr. Evans," Dr. Donald called out.

Rachel shuddered.

She didn't know if she wanted to go back to the stream after what had occurred last night. It would be like returning to the scene of the crime, a painful reminder of her one wild hair that had gotten out of hand. A picture of her gun flashed in her mind.

On second thought…

She finished her coffee and headed in the direction of the stream. In the daylight the trail was much easier to traverse. Soft vegetation and century old trees all wrapped around each other trying to choke the life from one another in a fight for survival. She reached the water's edge and looked around—the pistol was nowhere to be found.

Rachel skirted the rim of the trees, pushing aside plants and shrubs, but still no gun. She was about to turn and head back up the trail when something caught her attention.

She crouched and moved the lush grass aside. In the mud, as plain as day, was a smudged footprint. A very large, oversized man's bare footprint. She stood and placed her own booted foot inside the impression.

The print dwarfed her foot by at least eight inches.

Chills rolled down her spine and up her arms, leaving goosebumps. She felt blood drain from her face as she gazed at the deceptively peaceful looking jungle. The giant shadowy figure from last night flashed through her mind.

She glanced down at the print. *Someone — or something — is out there...*

And now it has a gun.

Rachel returned to the camp, her nerves on edge. She walked straight across the clearing to Dr. Rumsinger.

"I need to have a word with you." Rachel pulled off her ball cap and ran a shaky hand through her tangled hair.

Donald scowled. "Can't it wait, Evans? I'm busy."

"No, Professor it can't." Her voice firmed as she eyed the ruddy-faced man with disdain.

He waved his hand in an impatient gesture. "Well then, out with it and make it snappy. We should have been gone from here an hour ago."

Rachel took a deep breath before launching into her cause for concern. "I found a footprint down by the water. And last night...I think someone entered my tent."

The Professor shrugged his heavy shoulders. "Really, Dr. Evans, that's no surprise. A dozen or so men have already been down by the water doing their morning ablutions." He curled his thick lips back and sneered in disgust. "As for your personal habits, I don't want to hear about your secret liaisons."

Rachel rolled her eyes. "This isn't a joke, Professor. I'm serious."

"Was it an animal?" He glanced over his glasses. "You know there are a lot of species here in the jungle."

"I realize that." Her voice rose in pitch as her patience fell away. "It wasn't that kind of print...at least I don't think it was." Rachel brought her hand to her forehead, rubbing it back and forth as she considered the

59

possibilities. The print had been smeared. Was she overreacting?

"Would you like to know what I discovered?" Donald's eyes sparked fire, then he frowned and pulled Rachel's pistol from one of his pockets. "You're irresponsible, Dr. Evans. And you are wasting my time."

Rachel flushed with embarrassment. Just her luck, of all the people who could have found her gun, Donald was the one. Before she could reach out and grab the pistol, the Professor snatched it up and slipped it back into his pocket, patting the barrel for good measure.

"You were saying?"

Rachel cleared her throat. "The p-print was large." She twisted her fingers. "About two and a half to three sizes larger than my foot."

The Professor glanced down at Rachel's feet, then back at her face and sniffed. "It wouldn't take much to be larger than your feet, Dr. Evans. Now, I really must get back to work. We're out of here in ten minutes. Stop acting like a hysterical female. I expect professionalism on this expedition." With that said, he turned on his heel and left her standing with her mouth agape.

"Asshole," she muttered under her breath.

"What was that, Dr. Evans?" he said over his shoulder.

"Nothing."

"I didn't think so."

Rachel's palms hurt from her nails digging into them. She gritted her teeth until her jaw ached, then returned to oversee the dismantling of her tent. But not before flipping the bird at the bastard's arrogant backside.

* * * * *

They had been hiking through the jungle for three hours when the Professor called for a break. Rachel was grateful, but would never tell him. She couldn't stand the "I told you so" look that would cross his pudgy face.

The pack on her back grew heavier, like a leaded weight, so much so she'd become convinced items had been added to the sack while she wasn't looking. Rachel shrugged it off her knotted shoulders and set it down on the ferns growing about her feet.

The tops of the trees swayed gently, rustling with a breeze, but the light wind didn't reach the jungle floor. Down here the air was musky, heavy, and damn near stifling. On the occasion that it did stir, Rachel caught the scent of orchids and lilies, although she had yet to see any of the elusive blooms.

Vines and lianas tangled their corded lengths around the tree trunks, in thick black ropes that looked like sprouting hair. Primordial tree ferns grew rampant, adding to the overall denseness of the jungle.

Rachel stretched her weary muscles. Her back hurt and her bones cracked as she moved her hips side to side. Her feet were aching from the blisters that had formed, worse than the time she'd tried to break in a pair of stilettos on Madison Avenue.

Jac and Brigit's faces danced before her eyes. They shook their heads, their expressions clearly taunting her with *I told you so*. Rachel stuck out her tongue at the imaginary images.

She'd show them. She wasn't a quitter.

Determination coursed through her tired veins. She swatted a mosquito. The little pests had probably already sucked a pint out of her. She was surprised she didn't feel faint from blood loss.

The natives pulled out bits of jerky, camu camu, and manioc from their packs and started chomping away. She looked longingly at the dry, salty meat and fresh fruit. Her stomach growled. She was sure somewhere in her pack an emergency stash of chocolate lay hidden. Maybe now was a good time to find the sweets.

Rachel bent over and started to search her pack when a brown hand stopped her. The man bringing up the rear pressed a slice of jerky in her palm, along with a camu camu fruit. She thanked him in his language, and then greedily ate the morsels.

Water canteens were passed around, and then, too soon, they were trekking through the tangled mass of growth once again.

The trail, if you could call it that, narrowed and the going slowed to almost a crawl. Guides with machetes hacked their way through thick lianas. Two hours and less than a mile later the vegetation changed. Plants thinned out a tiny bit and the leaves got larger.

Rachel stopped to examine a particularly distinctive purple leaf, her hands shaking from the effect of the caffeine-rich camu camu on her system. With a piece of that fruit a day, she'd never need another cup of coffee.

Breaking off the beefy purple leaf, she flipped it over and ran her trembling fingers along the veins in the center. Light fuzz covered the entire area. Water droplets lay captured in its tiny follicles.

Chills raced up her spine, as though she was being watched, and she quickly glanced over her shoulder. The jungle was still, eerily so. She searched the treetops for any sign of movement, but caught none. A sloth sat motionless a good fifty feet above her. But other than that creature, she saw nothing.

She rolled her shoulders in an attempt to ward off the unwanted sensation and brought her attention back to the plant in her hands.

Something wasn't right. This plant wasn't right. It shouldn't be here.

At that moment Rachel knew that this whole expedition was a bad idea. She lifted her head, searching for her colleague. "Dr. Donald, come take a look at this."

He stiffened, hesitating for a second. Anger twisted his face into a macabre mask as he stomped back to where she stood, crushing several fragile ferns in his path. "If you can't keep up, you'll be left behind."

Rachel shot him a heated look.

The Professor's eyes narrowed, but he said nothing. He looked at the leaf in her hands, then snatched it away for a closer examination. He turned the plant over, staring at it for a few minutes, before declaring, "I'll be damned."

"What is it?"

"This plant is supposed to be extinct."

"I thought so, but as you know my specialty is not botany."

"This particular plant was declared extinct over two hundred year ago," Donald remarked.

Rachel smiled. She had her sample to take back to show the board. Her promotion guaranteed.

The Professor looked over his shoulder to the men and motioned for one to join him. "Bag a sample and we'll bring it along."

A large native man with black eyes walked forward. He lowered the pack from his brown muscled back and took out a bag.

Rachel stopped the native's actions by placing her hand over the top of his. "Professor don't you think I should carry the leaves? After all, I found them."

Donald looked down at her hand and then into her face. His eyes flashed fire. "We're all in this together, my dear." He sneered and patted her gun in his pocket. A quick nod told the man to continue.

The native pulled his hand from Rachel's and carefully snipped another leaf from the plant. Rachel's face burned as the native slipped the sample into a plastic bag, along with the one the Professor had been holding. He dropped both into his pack and then hefted the pack onto his shoulders and they headed off again.

Rachel bit the inside of her cheek so hard she drew blood. Donald planned to take credit for her discovery. She'd been so naïve to think he'd actually let her get an ounce of credit on this expedition. Once again, she hadn't anticipated this level of devious behavior from him.

Every time she thought he'd sunk as low as he could possibly go, the bar would drop again. That's fine. He could keep this sample for himself. She didn't need it. There'd be other discoveries. She decided that the next item she came across she'd keep for herself. It would be her little secret.

Rachel studied the variety of flora and fauna as she hiked through the jungle. It was amazing what grew under the thick canopy, considering how little sunlight reached the floor. Cat's Claw plants were all over the jungle floor, along with lemon grass and gray fungus. Ginger flowers as tall as a shrub bloomed with beautiful red petals.

Monkeys played amongst the trees, swinging from vine to vine, using their tails and hands. She caught glimpses of red and gray fur with each flurry of movement. Parrots with brightly colored blue, yellow, and purple feathers flittered overhead, their squawks so loud at times she couldn't hear herself think. The area was magnificent in its primal splendor.

She wondered what else could be in this jungle that should have been extinct years ago. She shuddered as she recalled the massive print in the mud. Bigfoot flashed in her mind, before she rolled her eyes at her own foolishness. It wasn't that mythical creature, but something far more dangerous to her senses.

Long blond hair, a massive chest, shadowy features and heated caresses flashed through her mind. She flushed as she recalled his tongue buried deep within her body, devouring her.

Could it have been a dream? But it seemed so real.

Rachel stopped for a second, closed her eyes and bit down on her lip to keep from groaning. She tried in vain to shut off the rush of sensation washing over her. She blinked, willing herself to face reality, not fantasy.

He forced you, remember?

She snorted. It hadn't taken much persuasion on his part. She'd opened for him quicker than the doors at a New York Barneys' sale. Rachel felt her panties dampen as she imagined what the rest of the god's body looked like.

Exactly like the man in the erotic dreams she'd been having back at home. She shook her head to clear the carnal thoughts.

It has to be jungle fever.

He couldn't have been real.

It was afternoon by the time they reached the mouth of a large muddy river. The water looked deceptively calm on the surface, but mini whirlpools breaking the top told otherwise. The shore held bits of gold and rock that had washed up from the running water.

Not enough to get rich, Rachel thought, *just enough to fire greed.*

The men shuffled their feet in unease. Heated words were exchanged as the native guides pointed at the black waterway and shook their heads. Their whispers carried tales of a deadly undercurrent, gigantic snakes and fanged monsters. Several of the men stepped away from the water, shaking their shaven heads, refusing to go in.

Dr. Donald bellowed at the lead guide in charge of the men, making it perfectly clear what he expected to get for his money.

She couldn't hear everything being said from her position toward the back of the line, but saw the men glance in her direction a couple of times.

The Professor's face glowed red as he pushed his way to where Rachel stood. "It seems, my dear, these superstitious bastards are refusing to cross."

Rachel looked over Donald's shoulder to the group of men. "What has them so spooked?"

Donald arched a brow. "Apparently they believe a fierce tribe lives on the other side of the river and that if we cross we'll all die." He shrugged as if that were no big deal.

She couldn't quite hide the curiosity in her voice. "What kind of tribe?" Rachel took a step forward, not wanting to miss a word.

"I haven't been able to get much out of the men. They keep jabbering about ghosts and a sacrifice. They seem to think by talking about the mythical tribe, it will actually bring them to us, or some rubbish like that," he blustered.

"A sacrifice?"

"You know — probably the usual virgin sacrifice. Care to volunteer, Dr. Evans?" He smirked and raised an eyebrow as if he seriously considered giving her to the guides.

"Sorry, Professor. I don't qualify," Rachel bit out, meeting his gaze evenly.

His face flushed, making it almost purple against his ruddy complexion. "The men believe we're being followed as we speak. You may want to watch your back."

It was Rachel's turn to feel ill. She looked over her shoulder at the peaceful jungle and went from hot to cold in seconds. *Was her dream man here?* She'd had a feeling that something had changed when they came upon that plant.

Call it woman's intuition, or just plain city girl mugger smarts. She should have insisted they turn back then. She just didn't want her overactive imagination costing her the promotion she'd worked so hard to get.

Donald cleared his throat and placed an awkward hand on her shoulder, the touch light and fleeting, far from comforting. Just as quickly, he snatched it back as if afraid he'd catch something from the miniscule contact. "I want you to speak with them. You know their dialect. Reason with them."

The Professor's words brought her out of her haze. "I'm not sure that's such a good idea." She glanced to where the men were gathered. They were eyeing her strangely. She shook off the sudden premonition and turned to the Professor. "If they're trying to warn us, maybe we should listen."

"Your specialty is ancient languages and cultures, yes?"

"It is but—"

"But nothing. You listen to me. If you want to have a chance in hell of getting your promotion, Dr. Evans, you'll get over there and convince them everything is fine." His face twisted into a ghoulish expression of disgust. "Remember, I'm the one who will fill out the report when we return to New York."

Rachel's shoulders slumped. She had no choice but to do what Dr. Donald demanded.

She walked to Jaro, the native guide who was in charge. In a calm voice she told him that if they did not cross the river, the fat man with the red hair was not only going to punish them by not paying, but planned on hurting her, too.

Black eyes shot in the direction of the Professor. The native guide's gaze narrowed to daggers before releasing a slew of words to the other workers. Rachel cringed at the rapid fire of his angry dialect. He'd demanded that the packs be picked up and hauled to the other side of the river.

He looked down one last time into Rachel's face. For a second she thought she saw lust in the black depths, but it dissolved so quickly she figured she must have been mistaken.

The group walked further down the muddy shoreline. The river narrowed and appeared to be passable. The first three guides went into the murky water, carrying the packs on their heads. The swirling torrents hit them about chest high, causing a rough wake to fan out behind them.

The men kept a watchful eye on the water, looking for anything out of the ordinary. All three made it safely to the other side and signaled for everyone to follow.

Rachel squinted against the sunlight on her face, enjoying the fluffy clouds floating blissfully on the breeze. This was the first time she'd gotten an unobstructed view of the sky. She'd missed the sun.

She was second to last in line when she stepped into the river, holding her pack over her head. The water was up to her chin by the time she reached the halfway mark. If it got any deeper, she'd have to swim for it.

Her arms trembled beneath the weight of the pack. The stones on the riverbed were slick with moss, making her footing less than sure. Rachel stepped carefully, knowing that if she slipped she'd probably drown.

Finally, she reached the far shore and turned to see the last guide crossing with his pack above his head. He was halfway across when his face drained of color. No one seemed to notice but Rachel, because everyone was too busy checking their packs and equipment. She scanned the water, but couldn't make out anything unusual.

He screamed, "Anaconda!" in his native language.

All chatter stopped.

The horror filled sound reverberated off the distant cliffs, bouncing against the trees, finally muting against the swirling water. The pack flew out of his hands and rapidly floated down stream as he started to run the rest of the distance to shore.

His eyes were wide and his nostrils flared as he tried to suck in enough air to fuel his flight. He made it ten more feet before something unseen and stealth-like grabbed him from beneath the water and pulled him down.

His last cry was cut short as his head was sucked under. For a few moments water churned where he'd been standing, before returning to its deceptively calm exterior.

Rachel heard a distant scream that seemed to grow louder with each passing moment. The cry sounded wounded and animalistic. She strained to focus on the direction, but was unable.

The Professor appeared before her, flushed with anger. He drew back his hand and slapped her.

The screaming stopped.

* * * * *

Eros's eyes narrowed and his muscles bunched, ready for action. After the joining ceremony, the second Eros got the opportunity he'd kill the fire-haired bastard for striking his woman. He cursed, as renewed anger surged through him. He couldn't risk taking the man's life now and destroying the sacredness of the ceremony. He gripped the liana in his hand as if it were a lifeline, the only thing keeping him from making good on his promise right now.

His heart clenched as he watched her horror-filled eyes take in the death of the native. He'd give anything to be able to sweep the memory from her, and return the smile she'd given him last night.

Soon he'd get his chance...

Chapter Five

Rachel was numb. Her senses dull, the colors around her muted by the tears in her eyes. She followed the guides through the dense underbrush, no longer caring whether they stopped for breaks or walked on forever. She'd just seen a man die.

She brought up the rear now, stumbling over exposed roots, tripping on tangled vines and snuffing the life out of delicate ferns. Her mind tried to make sense of what had occurred at the river.

The water flowed, just like the stream she'd swam in the night before.

It could have just as easily been her that the snake chose to attack, not some poor guy trying to make a buck.

She tried to picture the native man's face. His rough features blurred and morphed every time she thought she was close to seeing them. She wondered if he'd even had a chance to take a wife. Maybe he'd never been married, never had kids.

And now he never would.

A tear streaked down her face and landed on her hand. The drop blended in with the sheen of perspiration covering her skin. Her chest ached. She didn't want to go through life without having someone to love, someone who'd love her back. And maybe, just maybe, kids. She sniffed, trying to hold back the flow of tears.

It didn't work. Somewhere inside her a dam had broken. All the pain and frustration she'd experienced over the last few years flowed out, leaving a salty trail behind.

She swiped a grubby hand across her face, trying to wipe away the moisture. Her eyes were blurring so bad that she couldn't see the trail. Frustrated, she stopped. The caravan of men kept going, which was fine with her. She needed a minute alone to compose herself.

Rachel shrugged the pack off and reached inside for a hanky. She didn't want to leave any litter, so she'd passed on bringing tissues. She grabbed the clean cloth and dabbed at her eyes.

She spied a fallen tree about five yards away that looked inviting. Rachel dragged her backpack over to the mossy green trunk and sat down. The air was hot, muggy and all around unpleasant.

Jac and Brigit were right. She wasn't ready for a real expedition, one where people died. She needed her friends, needed to talk to them. She needed to get the hell out of this jungle.

Rachel glanced at the trail. The caravan disappeared out of sight and she couldn't hear the rustling of feet. Something inside her told her she should be worried, but she wasn't.

She looked at her watch, her mind scrambled, trying to calculate the time difference. Digging in her bag, she pulled out her cell phone, praying the GPS would work in this thick canopy. She punched in the numbers, almost by rote, since the sun barely permeated the green depths.

The line crackled and hissed, but then she heard the distinct sound of ringing. Her heart leapt.

"Pick up, pick up, Jac. Please pick up."

"Hello."

"Jac, it's me, Rachel. Can you hear me?"

"I can't come to the phone right now, but if you leave me a message I'll get back to you as soon as possible — if you're lucky."

Rachel's spirits sank, swallowed up by the moist earth below her feet. She heard several beeps on the end of the line before a final long beep signaled her turn to speak.

"Jac, it's me. I just wanted you to know that I miss you guys and I can't wait to come back home." Rachel scrubbed tears from her cheek with her palm. "You were right. Right about everything. I'll try to call later when we make caaaahhhhh — "

A big hand reached from behind her and covered her mouth. A man's hand. Rachel tried to break loose and scream, but it was no use. The hand didn't budge. Instead, the man grabbed her hanky and shoved it in her mouth. A thin vine looped over the top of the hanky, cutting off all chance of yelling for help.

She clenched the cell phone in her hand and hurriedly pressed off with her thumb, before shoving the phone into her pocket. She didn't want her friend to hear the last gasps of life leave her body.

She felt herself being lifted from behind. Rachel scratched and kicked frantically against her assailant, fighting like an animal possessed. Several more hands grasped her, tying her feet and wrists as she struggled.

Rachel recognized Jaro, the guide she'd been talking to earlier. *What is he doing?*

Several of the men from the expedition stood around her. She'd been trussed like a turkey by the time they'd finished. From the looks on their startled faces, she'd at least gotten a few good jabs in.

Serves them right.

Fear seeped into her bones, weighing them down like a marble slab. She was defenseless. They could do anything they wanted to her and she wouldn't be able to do a thing about it. Her heart lurched.

In her mind, she tried to remember how many guides were on the expedition. Fifteen…twenty…enough for a very efficient gang rape. New York Times articles sprung into her mind about group violence. *Wilding*, they'd called it.

Her stomach flipped and bile rose in her throat. She screamed against the gag, her body tensing and straining, testing the strength of her restraints. The vines bit into her tender wrists. She felt the warm trickle of liquid drip down her hand.

Blood. Her blood.

Rachel's head began to swim. If she were lucky she'd lose consciousness before they had a chance to touch her.

The guides began to chant ritualistic words, their voices strangely hypnotic in cadence, yet terrifying considering the situation. A familiar voice bellowed out. The blood in her veins froze.

The Professor, where was he? He'd stop all this nonsense at once, if she could just get his attention.

Dr. Donald stepped into her line of vision. "I told you my dear, in order to get the natives to continue on, there must be a sacrifice. You don't mind that I mentioned to them that they could take you, do you?"

Rachel's eyes bugged out and she tried to kick and scream at the bastard, to no avail. The vines were too tight.

He chuckled. "I'll take that as a no."

Her heart sank. *He was part of it. Hell, he was the reason for them tying her up.*

The asshole had sacrificed her. Shock, fear, and revulsion crashed through her until all that remained was white-hot anger. Rachel narrowed her eyes to razor slits.

I'll get you for this, if I ever get out of here alive. And if I don't, I'll haunt you straight to hell.

The Professor turned to Jaro.

"I think she's mad at me," he smirked. "Make it quick. This part of the jungle gives me the creeps." He rubbed his arms as if to ward off a chill, then turned on his heel and walked away, leaving her at the mercy of the native men.

Rachel watched his retreating back until he was out of sight, her eyes burning with angry tears. She blinked them back, then glared at Jaro.

He'd also observed the Professor's hasty retreat, and a look of disgust crossed his coffee colored features. His black orbs returned to Rachel, a half smile covering his brown face. Without words, she pleaded with him.

"Perhaps I have time to show you what a real man is like. I'm sure the gods wouldn't mind if I test you first, before sending you off to meet them," Jaro grumbled, rubbing his hand along his cock through the front of his pants.

Rachel watched in horror as his rod began to lengthen and stir. The men around her laughed and egged Jaro on. The pungent sweat of their bodies choked off the air. Rachel struggled, her boots kicking up bits of dirt from the ground. Revulsion slithered through her blood like thousands of tiny fire ants.

"I think you'd like that, wouldn't you?" Jaro crouched in front of her, reached out and pinched her nipple, twisting until pain shot through Rachel's body.

She screamed against the gag once again.

"Maybe I'll take that rag out of your mouth and put those pretty lips to use sucking my dick. I bet you'd be good." The menacing smile on his face made her skin crawl.

Rachel watched Jaro raise his hand to his zipper, freeing his brown cock. He grasped his rod, whipping it from side-to-side in front of her face like a sword. Taunting, a not so subtle reminder of exactly what he planned to do to her.

"I can tell you're hungry for me." He cupped her cunt. "I bet if I cut your pants off you'd be wet." He made a move as if to make good on his promise.

Rachel shook her head and struggled violently against her bonds. She could feel the veins bulging in the side of her neck.

Jaro's expression turned cold and he shoved his penis back into his pants. His black eyes bore into hers, sparking with barely contained rage.

"So you think you're too good for me?" He spit on the ground beside her face. "You had your chance." Jaro lifted a wooden rainbow painted club above his head. The singsong chanting resumed and increased in volume.

Rachel knew she was going to die. Colors collided. Her vision swam.

He brought the club down swiftly and thankfully her world went black.

Chapter Six

Eros's heart froze when he saw the native raise the ceremonial club in the air. He'd been following the expedition for the past several miles looking for a place to snatch his woman. He'd taken the time to scout ahead and now because of his absence she was about to lose her life before his eyes.

He bellowed, a cry of anguish ripping from his chest, echoing through the jungle. Monkeys screamed and scattered throughout the treetops. Birds flapped their wings in their hurry to escape. Insects stopped their busy noises.

He raised his large palm, pointing it in the direction of the man holding the club. Brilliant energy shot out, ripping the weapon from the man's grasp, searing the native's hand. The guide screamed, clutching the burned limb.

The natives stepped away from Rachel's limp body and scattered. As they ran away, their panicked voices shouted about the fierce ghost tribe.

Eros jumped down from the tree he'd been perched in, and ran a shaky hand through his long hair. His fingers trembled as the excess energy was absorbed back into his system.

He approached the woman slowly, carefully, his body as sensitive to his surroundings as an exposed nerve in a loose tooth. Natural predators gave him a wide berth, sensing the danger.

She lay bound, her sable hair thrown in disarray around her face from the struggle. Long lashes fell in soft crescents against her pale cheeks. The hat she'd worn sat amongst the leaves about ten feet from her small body.

He crouched and reached a fingertip out to move the stray locks from her forehead. She was warm. The breath from her pert nose came out even and deep. He picked her up as if she were the finest gem, brushing leaves away from her clothes and out of her hair.

Eros ran a hand over her, examining her for injuries. She'd be bruised if he didn't treat her. He sent energy through her, the heat permeating her body, healing her from the inside out.

It was time to take her home.

* * * * *

Rachel awoke in mid air, her arms and legs hanging limp. She must be floating up to heaven. At least she hoped she was. Her muscles were numb and sore from lack of circulation. The strange thing was her head didn't hurt.

She opened her eyes and caught a glimpse of large feet, then long legs, bulging biceps and a wide muscled chest.

Yep, definitely heaven.

Her eyes were drawn up and up and up. The man lifting her was a giant. At least he seemed like it to Rachel. The rainbow stick, the guides, the attack, being tied up. Flash by flash the pictures collided in her fuzzy mind. Rachel wriggled and thrashed.

The man held her with one hand, her feet dangling a foot off the ground as if she weighed no more than a rag doll. Her struggles went unnoticed. He pulled a huge knife from a sheath at his waist and sliced through the vines binding her hands and feet. He left her gag in place.

She squirmed, trying to break his hold, all the while knowing escape was futile. She looked into his face.

Rachel's breath seized.

His eyes, a rich shade of blue, held her gaze — locking her to him, drawing her in, arresting her until all thought of escape vanished like a dream upon waking. Undisguised desire flared from their aqua depths, promising, imploring, and beseeching.

He was lethal.

His features were starkly handsome, as if he'd been chiseled from Michelangelo's granite. Long sun-kissed hair hung wildly around his face and down his back, past his narrow hips. His lips were firm, but full. An inkling of familiarity danced across her mind.

Then it hit her. *This was her dream man.*

Except he wasn't a dream at all.

Rachel stilled, every fiber of her being honed in on his body. She reached out, unable to stop herself from touching his bare chest. She had to make sure he was real for her own peace of mind. Her fingers met with steeled warmth, and tingled on contact. He was a man of contrasts. Soft, yet hard. Tender, yet fierce.

Rachel pressed her palm flat, scraping his flat disc of a nipple.

He flinched. His blue gaze widened in surprise, then turned tumultuous like the ocean in the midst of a storm. Before she had a chance to speak, he flung her over his massive shoulder. The air rushed out of Rachel's lungs, leaving her gasping for breath behind the gag. The giant took off, racing through the jungle at an astonishing speed.

Rachel squirmed against his arm. She tried to untie the vine holding her gag in place, but her fingers weren't cooperating. She had to go back. She owed the Professor big time and wasn't about to let him get away without payback. *Let's see how he likes a gun shoved in his face.* Rachel needed to find her pack and the little *gift* from Jac she'd shoved in the bottom of it. That was the only way she'd be able to get out of this place alive and back home to New York.

She pounded on the man's back, hoping he'd let her go. It was like hitting concrete with a feather. Rachel bounced as he jumped over tree trunks and around vines. The ground zipped by in a blur of green.

Rachel concentrated on taking quick breaths, closing her eyes for a second to keep from getting sick. Her insides tossed and churned, like she'd been thrown into a human blender.

His large body was hot and slick with sweat and smelled of musk against the jungle air. Sliding against him reminded Rachel of intertwining bodies, skin on skin, and sex.

She willed herself to keep pummeling him. Her hands were red and hurt worse with each blow that fell. Sooner or later, he'd have to get tired of her attacks and let her go, or at least put her down.

The giant simply slapped her on the butt and kept running. Her eyes widened and she sucked in a surprised breath. She hadn't been spanked since she was a child. She tried to rise up to look at the side of his face, but her bottom throbbed and stung.

The heat radiating out from her rounded backside caused other things to stir. She chastised herself for being so foolish, yet her body continued to respond with an answering wetness between her thighs. Rachel clamped her legs together. Ashamed, but turned on, she wiggled again, hoping and fearing another quick slap.

You're being kidnapped by a giant, and instead of concentrating on freeing yourself, you're getting horny.

She hit him again, out of anger at herself. This time he stopped and pulled her off his shoulder. His eyes met hers and she cowered, waiting for the blow to come.

It never did.

Rachel tried to pull the gag from her mouth, but the knot was too tight. Her jaw ached. She eyed his imposing form. She'd give her lifesavings for a glass of water or *a king-sized bed.*

The giant stroked her hair, his manner soothing, then swiftly snatched a bit of vine from a tree, spun her around, and bound her hands behind her back.

Rachel strained, trying to pull the ties apart. The position thrust her full breasts out, making her shirt gape open. She realized her awkward situation and stilled.

He circled her, a couple of times sniffing the air, like a wolf scenting prey. Her skin prickled with awareness as she observed him from beneath her lashes. His nostrils flared as his eyes wandered over her in a slow appreciative perusal, coaxing, leading and drawing out a response.

Everywhere he looked, she burned. He paused at her nipples as they beaded under her white T-shirt. He growled deep in his belly. His tongue darted out to lick his bottom lip.

Oh god, he can smell my arousal.

Her traitorous body responded, as she remembered that dangerous tongue from last night. Rachel now knew it had been no dream—it was every bit as real as the man standing before her. He'd fucked her with that wet, smooth, powerful muscle. And dammit, she would let him do it again in a heartbeat.

The material of his loincloth rose with the evidence of his desire.

She couldn't draw her eyes away from the outline of his massive cock. Her breathing deepened and there was no fighting the attraction. She ached with need.

Rachel imagined his muscle bound body moving on top of her, spreading her thighs, sliding inside, filling her with a cock so long and thick that she'd feel it in the back of her throat by the time he got done fucking her.

She groaned, knowing in the end she would surrender and scream out in ecstasy. *Just like I did last night.*

Her expression must have been obvious, for he smiled, flashing startlingly white teeth against his tanned face. The look he gave her was positively feral.

* * * * *

Eros fought the urge to rut with his woman here on the jungle floor. Her thoughts were driving him to madness. His cock ached from the long hours of thinking about her touching his body, torturing his mind, without being able to do anything about it. If he hadn't snatched her undergarment last night, he wouldn't have made it through the night without acting upon his base desires.

But the seer must perform the ceremony first. It was the only way to ensure his fertility.

Rachel's breasts quivered under his gaze and her nipples beaded. She recalled their intimate joining and he could smell her wetness without having to see or feel it.

Eros looked up to the sky, begging the goddess for strength. Her guidance was the only way he was going to be able to make it to the village without ravishing the woman.

He glanced down at her flat stomach. Their child would soon ripen in her belly, completing the prophecy. That same child, while still in her womb, would possess enough energy to start the transport, leading his people to the new world beyond the stars. Their future babe held the key to his people's happiness.

Eros took a deep breath to calm his raging hormones. He would wait, until the moment was right and then claim what was rightfully his.

If she would only cooperate and stop tempting him.

He swung her up and threw her over his shoulder, positioning her for the next run. His long fingers lingered on her backside, stroking lightly but avoiding her sex, for what felt like an eternity. Rachel's pussy was drenched by the time he slid his hand down to rest on her thighs.

Damn him. He knew exactly what he was doing to her.

Her insides jarred with each step he took, and she fought for air. Something hard bit into her thigh and she shifted, trying to gain a more comfortable position. The object in her pocket slid down further and Rachel recalled she'd put her cell phone there during the attack.

She didn't need her pack after all.

She would have smiled, but the gag had drained every ounce of moisture from her mouth, making it impossible to swallow without a sharp dry pain following. He had one arm slung around her, holding her in place. Silky hair brushed the side of her face, sending shivers of awareness through her hungry body.

From her upside down position she took in his well-rounded backside as he made his way deeper into the thick growth. The animal hide loincloth barely covered his luscious cheeks. She coughed against the gag.

This man has a fine ass.

Muscles flexed and lengthened with his stride. His legs were unusually long and his feet were left uncovered. They were oversized, just like the prints she'd seen in the mud at base camp.

*He was there that night at the stream…*watching.

A mixture of fear and excitement coursed through her at the realization. He'd seen her naked. She'd made him groan.

Oh, great, just what I need. A horny Tarzan-like giant holding me captive.

She was getting tired of this caveman crap. Didn't he know it went out a long time ago? The ground rushed by at blinding speed. She prayed he didn't drop her, because from this height it would definitely hurt.

She rested her face against his back, his skin soft against her cheek. He was deeply tanned, but a slightly different shade of brown than the native guides. His skin held a golden hue, almost as if it had been fair at one time.

Interesting…

Rachel searched her mind for a tribe that would have his characteristics, but none in this equatorial vicinity came to mind. No matter, she was sure that once he removed the gag she'd be able to communicate with him and clear this whole mess up.

Chapter Seven

The sun was setting when they reached a tiny clearing. It would be dark in an hour or so. The last of the gold beams waltzed with the outstretched shadows. The wild man had been running for hours. Any normal man would have dropped from exhaustion by now, but not her giant.

He carefully pulled her off his shoulder and set her down, steadying her with his hands, waiting until her legs had enough strength to support her weight. He unsheathed his knife and cut the vines from her mouth and hands, replacing the blade when he'd finished.

Rachel tried to spit the gag out but couldn't. She grasped the hanky and tugged it from her parched mouth. Her whole body hurt, from head to toe. The giant reached out and clasped her right hand within his own larger callused ones and began to rub it vigorously, until the impressions from the vines faded and her fleshy pink color returned.

Satisfied with the first, he repeated his ministrations with her left hand. The heat generated from his fingers astonished Rachel, and for a second she thought she actually saw them glow. But it must have been a trick of the fading light.

She took a step away from him and looked up. She could see him better, now that his hair was slick with sweat and swept back from his face. Rachel sucked in a startled breath. He'd make the Calvin Klein models green with envy. He was a golden-tressed god.

His beauty stunned Rachel speechless. Not that she could have said anything at that moment with her throat drier than the Mojave.

The giant put his hands together in front of his mouth. A strange whistle-like sound occurred, even though he didn't appear to be blowing out air. Birds stopped chattering and the monkeys stilled.

A few moments of silence passed and then an answering call pierced the quiet. He made two more consecutive noises that were answered in kind. Then he reached down and picked her up and they were off.

Rachel's body felt bruised and battered. She wanted to just stay in one place for a while until the continuous rocking motion stopped. They reached another section of thick jungle, and this time he slowed to a walk.

Thank goodness. It's about time.

She was pretty sure she had a bruise on her hip from where the phone had been digging into her earlier. His hand rested on her legs, stroking her soothingly, as he strode into some kind of semi-cleared encampment. From her awkward position Rachel could see about thirty-to-forty people peeking out from behind trees, their gazes curious but not alarmed. They looked similar to the man carrying her, unusually tall, well built—all blonde, blue-eyed and beautiful.

Just my luck, I've been kidnapped by Amazons, she thought wryly.

Her eyes fell upon a large man, as dark as the others were fair. His jet-black hair hung past his waist, a leather strap around his forehead holding it away from his fierce face. His jade colored eyes followed them, boring holes right through her with their icy countenance. He was beautiful also, in a harsh, don't want to meet him in a back alley, sort of way.

Rachel shuddered.

The man frightened her. There was something dangerous about him. She decided it best not to ever piss him off.

The dark-haired man looked up, his gaze moving from hers to the giant who carried her. His face relaxed, as an unspoken understanding passed between the two men. The jade-eyed man nodded, then silent as a predator he turned and strode out of her line of sight.

Rachel tried to look around, but it was difficult given her upside-down position. Her ears were buzzing from the blood rushing to her head. If he set her down too fast she was pretty sure she'd pass out.

Her eyes continued to search the faces of the strange tribe. There didn't seem to be many women visible, which was strange, but not necessarily unusual. They probably considered *her* a threat.

She wanted to laugh as she imagined her five foot two self being any kind of threat against these giant people. The kids were probably taller than her at birth.

Where were all the children?

The giant carried her to the far end of the compound, then stopped. He made a big production out of gently placing her in a hand woven bark basket, as big as a VW Beetle, his head held high and his arms spread wide. He looked at the curious faces, making eye contact with all before he stepped in behind her.

Rachel couldn't miss his obvious display and the strange act had her insides twisting into knots. She wasn't sure of the meaning behind his behavior, but knew she wouldn't be staying long enough to find out. She had to get away, escape this place, these people.

Rachel wasn't exactly sure what she'd gotten herself into, but had the distinct impression she'd gone from the frying pan into the fire.

* * * * *

Eros's eyes met Ares, the dark warrior hunter, as the basket started to rise. It had been a while since Eros had seen his friend. Ares had chosen to live apart from the tribe many moon risings ago. Eros smiled, genuinely happy to see him.

Linking telepathically with Ares, Eros explained what had happened to his future mate. *I want the red-devil dead. I will form a hunting party and we will set out at dawn for —*

Ares stopped Eros's mental tirade by addressing him formally. *My King, what if you're unable to locate his trail? Let me take care of the red-haired man for you, if he is out there I will find him. You know you cannot kill him, without it destroying the sacredness of your upcoming ceremony.*

Eros's brows furrowed.

Ares continued. *I am unmated, so therefore not needed here in the village. I will check in with you often, updating you with my progress. You must stay and ensure your mate carries your babe within her belly. We cannot afford to lose you at this very crucial time. The entire village is counting on you.*

Ares's eyes met Eros with firm resolve. Eros realized there was no talking his friend out of this mission.

Be well, my brother. Eros watched Ares fade into the jungle.

* * * * *

Blood rushed from Rachel's head to her limbs, leaving her dizzy. She started to climb out, but stopped as she felt the basket lift off the ground. Rachel pushed her back as far against the side as possible to keep the basket from tipping.

Rachel tried to talk, but all that came out was a strangled cough. She needed water. She had no idea where he was taking her, but prayed the basket was sturdier than it looked.

The basket creaked and swayed under their weight. The vine holding it precariously in the air looked well worn. Rachel could see through cracks in the woven floor, the ground growing further and further away. Her heart began to pound and her palms started to sweat. *How high was this thing going to go?*

The contraption continued to climb to the tops of the trees. *Breathe, just remember to breathe.*

Rachel stared at the branches, trying to focus on the outstretched limbs. The thick growth swayed in the breeze, camouflaging several huts. She tried to ignore the frightening noises the conveyance made as she imagined her and the golden god plunging to their deaths.

The basket stopped with a jerk. Her heart dropped to her knees. The giant stepped out and then reached down to help her. His strong arms enveloped her, bringing her nose within two inches of his wide Adonis-like chest. His skin was soft and damp from the long run. She watched a stray bead of sweat make its way down his neck, between the flat disk-like nipples, over his taut abdomen, before disappearing under his loincloth.

Rachel inhaled. *Lucky droplet.*

His musky male fragrance sent her senses into overdrive. She had an uncontrollable urge to taste him, to run her tongue along his chest and lap up his salty essence.

He pulled her forward, snapping her out of her carnal thoughts.

Rachel shook her head. She'd heard that sometimes when people were in stressful situations they found themselves developing feelings for the people that put them there. *It must be Stockholm Syndrome.*

Rachel took one shaky step onto a wooden platform, and then looked down.

Big mistake.

They were up about sixty feet off the ground and she'd always been afraid of heights. She lunged for the giant, wrapping her small body around his waist, clinging to him for all she was worth.

He threw his head back and laughed. A loud billowy sound that made his non-existent belly shake against her straining arms. The deep baritone sent delicious shivers up her spine.

Eros looked down into the face of his petite woman. She tried hard to hide her fear, but her wide-eyed expression gave her away. He watched her as they reached the tops of the trees. Her small body quaked, even after she had thrown herself into his arms.

He longed to continue to hold her, to alleviate her fears, but the start of the ceremony had to be completed first. So Eros reluctantly pulled her tiny body away and led her to his hut. She had to enter willingly or the ceremony would be stopped before it could begin.

Eros pushed aside the sable-colored hide that covered the entrance to his hut. He entered and lowered his head. He offered all that he had, all that he was, to this enticing little woman. He'd give her his life if she asked for it. Eros would do anything and everything in his power to make her happy, if only she'd accept his nonverbal invitation.

Rachel stood outside the door. The giant stepped through the doorway, but hadn't tried to force her to join him. He waited patiently inside the hut, his eyes downcast. His face unreadable, but her gut said this moment was important to him.

She debated whether to enter. Different tribes had different customs. Sometimes actions even as innocent as stepping over a threshold made you married in the eyes of a tribe. Rachel looked over her shoulder at the drop behind her, and realized she didn't have a choice. She wasn't getting down that way.

With that thought, Rachel took a step forward.

His gaze shot up and he smiled, nodding his head in approval. His muscles visibly relaxed and he expelled the breath she hadn't noticed he'd been holding.

Suddenly she felt as if her fate had been sealed. Her gut clenched as panic crept into her body. There were no bars on the windows or solid doors, but she was as trapped as any prisoner could be. She had to breathe. Relax and breathe.

There had to be a way out of this situation. Rachel ran her hands through her tangled hair, catching each knot with her fingers, before slapping her palms onto her thighs. Her fingers nicked the phone.

Careful not to draw his attention, she wiped her hands nervously along her pants. She glanced around the hut. The walls were thatched, as was the roof, intricately woven with patterns that added a subtle Celtic-like design. Random beams of fading sunlight danced through the slotted windows, illuminating the tiny yet comfortable room. Hides of various shades were thrown on the wood floor, so many in fact that they reached close to eight inches high.

This is where he sleeps. The thought burned in her mind.

Rachel blushed and shot him a sideways glance, but he didn't flinch. He just watched her closely as she assessed the hut, as if waiting to see her reaction.

"It's nice," she croaked and nodded, looking around some more.

There was a bucket carved out of a tree stump in the corner, containing some kind of liquid. The giant grunted again and pointed to it, motioning for her to drink. Rachel walked to the corner and leaned over the bucket.

She sniffed a couple times, but smelled nothing. She didn't think he would try to poison her, but she wasn't sure what tribe she was dealing with. They didn't fit any of her research data.

Her raw throat throbbed with thirst. Rachel dipped a finger in and found the liquid surprisingly cool, like it had been refrigerated. That would have been no small feat considering the outside temperature.

She cupped her hands together in the liquid and lifted the wetness to her mouth. Her parched throat made it painful to swallow. Rachel turned to the man and smiled, wiping water droplets from her chin with the back of her hand.

He returned her smile and Rachel's heart sped.

She took a couple more drinks, soothing her dryness, then turned to face the giant. She'd drink more water in a few minutes, once she was sure the liquid would stay down. It was time to find out who these people were and explain to them why she needed to get out of here.

"My name is Dr. Rachel Evans," she said in the most common local dialect.

He stared at her as if she hadn't spoken. She tried eleven more regional languages before giving up. If he didn't speak any of the area dialects, then what language did he speak? Was he part of the mysterious lost tribe the native guides had spoken of?

She must be missing something. Perplexed, she walked the short distance to the hides and plopped down upon them. They were soft, welcoming, and surprisingly comfortable against her aching limbs. Exhausted from the long trek, she longed to stretch out and fall asleep.

Closing her eyes, she grabbed fistfuls of the fur, luxuriating in the down-like texture. Absently, Rachel wondered what they'd feel like against her naked skin.

She would slide the furs over her body, caressing her inner thighs until gooseflesh rose. She'd brush the thick blanket of hair along the edge of her nipples causing them to pucker in arousal.

Her breathing deepened, as her fingers kneaded the furs. Her mind turned to the dreams she'd been having in New York. They'd been so erotic, illicit—tantalizing like the man who'd brought her here. Rachel swallowed as she pictured his body against the furs. Hopefully before she left here she'd get the chance to see the real thing.

* * * * *

Eros watched Rachel examine his hut. He wanted her to like it, for it was her home now. Under veiled lashes he followed her movements as she drank from the water bucket, her pink tongue darting out to capture every last drop. He almost groaned aloud as he thought of all the ways he could put that tongue to use.

Guilt slashed at him. He should have stopped earlier and tended to her needs. His only thoughts had been to get her as far away from the group as possible.

And now she was here. The relief Eros felt was palpable. For a moment he had thought she would refuse to enter.

That she would refuse him.

His heart had quaked. The tension coiled tight, waiting to spring from his chest. He didn't think he could bear a moment more of the pressure. Then she'd stepped forward, over the threshold, and their destinies became intertwined.

Eros had blown out a shuddering breath. The first step completed. He could now go to the seer to find out who would be put in charge of readying his woman.

His jaw clenched at the thought. He did not like the new sensations that came from being around Rachel. Jealousy, the strongest and most violent emotion, was one he could have done without.

Eros watched her walk to his bed and sit on the furs. She stretched out as if she'd been there a thousand times before. Her delicate fingers grasped the furs. Her head was thrown back with her eyes closed, Eros imagined much like she would be in the throes of passion.

The expression on her face turned from one of exhaustion to desire within seconds. She continued to rub the furs against her hands, her restless body shifting slightly. Every part of Eros's body stood erect.

In his mind he saw his woman bare against the hides. Her rose colored nipples extended, the dewy thatch of curls in full view, as she spread her creamy thighs wide awaiting his shaft's arrival. Just like she'd been the night he'd visited her in her tent.

He grunted as his cock strained under his loincloth, searching for release. Eros reined in all of his control as he fought against his base nature. He labored to breathe and sweat broke across his brow.

The giant's grunt sounded strangled. It instantly brought her out of her musings. Rachel had forgotten that she wasn't alone. Her face felt warm, almost feverish, as her eyes sought his. His liquid gaze widened almost imperceptibly.

She glanced down at the furs, then back up into his face. The look he shot her was telling. He didn't need to say a word for her to know exactly what he was thinking.

Rachel flushed, her body tingling with awareness. She sprang off the bed as if it were on fire. Her tired muscles ached. Her traitorous mind tormented her with images of their writhing bodies, and she couldn't seem to stop her heart from racing.

His body shook and she could tell he fought for control. Need oozed from his every pore. He turned with effort and walked out the door, leaving her alone in the hut.

Rachel followed his retreating back until he'd disappeared. She had to get out of here. It was too dangerous for her to remain in this man's presence. He had her thinking insane thoughts.

She looked around the hut once more, not knowing how long it would be until he returned. Her body screamed for rest, but her mind wouldn't allow it.

Instead she reached into her pants pocket and pulled out her cell phone, her one and only lifeline to the outside world. She didn't know how long she had before he returned, so she punched in the numbers, determined to make this a quick call. She raised the receiver to her ear, getting an earful of static instead of a dial tone.

Shit.

Jac would be worried sick once she got Rachel's earlier message. She had to reach her friend, to tell Jac she was all right. But how?

Rachel pushed the off button on the cell phone. She'd try again tomorrow, if she got the chance, but for now she had to find a safe place to stash the phone. Her eyes fell on the thick pad of hides.

Rachel smiled and shoved the cell underneath. Hopefully the giant wouldn't sleep like the princess and the pea. She prayed he was like most men. If he were, then it would take weeks, if not months for him to find her phone. Not that she had to worry. She'd be out of here in a day or two.

With the GPS, Jac would be able to locate her general area and send in the Marines. Knowing Jac, that would mean she would come herself with a handful of armed men. Rachel bit her lip.

Heaven help the tribe if Jac has to come down to this jungle.

Chapter Eight

Eros swung from the edge of his hut to the seer's home, using one of the many vines lying snake-like amongst the branches. His cock ached and his palms itched to touch his woman.

She knew not the temptation she presented him. The mating ceremony must be performed before he could join with her, binding her to him completely. Two moons to go and the stars would be in alignment. He wasn't sure he'd survive 'til then. Ares stepped from the jungle, blocking his path.

"What ails you, my King?" Ares fought to hide a smile.

Eros groaned. "You know what ails me." His eyes narrowed and he shifted, unable to find comfort in the loincloth. "Wait until you encounter your mate, then we'll see who is laughing."

"My mate will surrender to the claiming and that will be the end of it." Ares nodded, certainty gleaming in his jade eyes.

Eros shook his head and smiled. "Just wait. The mighty Ares shall fall...hard. Have you found any trace of the red-devil?"

"No." Ares's jaw clenched. "But I'm not finished searching yet. Be well, my King." Ares clapped his hand on Eros's shoulder, then departed.

Eros reached the seer's door and psychically requested to enter, by raising his palm to the fur until it began to glow. Ariel raised the hide blocking her entrance and welcomed him inside.

Ariel smiled and nodded as she glanced at his loincloth. *I see your woman already affects you.*

Ariel's blonde curls hung past her waist, outlining her broad hips. She wore a traditional Atlantean outfit. Phosphorescent blue fabric draped low across her abdomen, highlighting her aqua eyes and displaying the top of her fleshy, hairless mound. Her breasts were full, plump and ripe as the richest melons.

I don't know if I can last until the ceremony, Eros lashed out psychically.

Stop yelling in my mind. You will wait, as all the males of our people have done before you.

What about Ares?

The seer's brows furrowed. *He is a different matter. Ares is one of us, but unusual. The bloodlines of his people have strict rules about taming their mates that he must follow. 'Tis not for us to interfere.*

Eros sighed. *I have waited so long.*

And you will wait longer. Your woman has not been prepared.

He fisted his hands in frustration. Eros didn't want any of the males of their tribe near his woman, even if it was just for the simple task of preparation. Goddess forbid, if his friend Ares was chosen. Not that he or Ares had a say in the matter, custom was custom.

Who has been given the task of final preparation?

*I have seen in my latest vision…*Ariel paused as her gaze met his.

Eros held his breath.

The corner of her mouth twitched at his obvious impatience. *It shall be you.*

"What?" he said aloud. His jaw dropped and surprise rang out from his deep voice.

Ariel clasped her hands patiently behind her back and lowered her gaze. "My visions are always clear, my King. 'Tis you who must prepare your woman for the ceremony."

"How can I touch her," his voice cracked with emotion as the muscles in his massive body flexed and tightened, "without claiming what is rightfully mine?"

"You will find a way." She shrugged and dismissed his concern with a slight wave of her hand. "Perhaps you can woo her." Ariel picked up the loose herbs on her table and dropped them into a cooking pot.

Eros slashed a hand through the air. "I've never had to *woo* anyone. This is my kingdom, I take what is mine." He slammed his palm down on the table, almost toppling the brew.

Ariel jumped, but said nothing for a few moments. She let out a slow breath and proceeded. "I fear if you try such with this woman, you will lose her, as well as the son I've prophesied. Do you wish that?"

"No!" Eros ran a shaking hand through his sweaty hair, and instantly it was clean.

"I've prepared the claiming rings for your pre-mating time. I must first apply yours, then you may apply your mate's." Ariel held up two gold hoops for Eros to view. "Are you ready for me to place them upon you?"

He nodded and sent a jolt of energy through his body to numb the skin. The seer clamped the first gold hoop through his right nipple. The second hoop pierced his left nipple a moment later. Eros sent another burst of energy through his body, healing the wounds as if they'd never existed.

"'Tis done," he confirmed, glancing down at the proof that showed the tribe he'd been claimed. His chest expanded, swelling with pride. The gold hoops glowed in the dim lighting, rasping his nipples with each exhalation.

"Very well then." She clapped her hands together. "Tonight you start." Ariel hesitated, before handing him another set of gold hoops.

Eros palmed the metal for a few seconds, feeling the cool rings caress his hand. Now all he had to do was convince his intended that piercing was part of the preparation. He didn't think that was going to go quite as smoothly.

He rolled the gold between his finger and thumb then placed them in a pouch on the side of his loincloth that contained Rachel's undergarment. His thoughts were turbulent as he imagined the fight ahead.

Ariel giggled.

His eyes narrowed, but he said nothing.

"To make sure you are in the right mindset, my King, I will relieve your discomfort."

Before Eros could respond, Ariel dropped to her knees before him. Her gentle fingers lifted his loincloth and untied the leather strap, freeing his straining cock. She slipped his staff into her mouth, wrapping her full lips around him and began to suck. Her hand closed around the base, gloving him, massaging, pumping.

Eros sunk his fingers into her thick hair for a few seconds, guiding her rhythmic movements. He closed his eyes as he imagined his woman, Rachel, on her knees before him. He saw her tentative smile as she took his length inside her welcoming mouth and sucked his cock, drawing out the seed. Eros pulled Ariel away, taking himself in hand. He needed his mate, not the seer.

He groaned as he envisioned Rachel's sable curls clutched in his hands. He'd gently guide her head up and down on his cock, while she took him deep inside her mouth. His breathing grew ragged and his balls drew up. At this rate he wouldn't last much longer. Eros squeezed the base of his cock, attempting to prolong the sweet misery. In his mind, he saw Rachel's pink tongue dart out and lick the length of him. That was all it took to send Eros over the edge.

His eyes flew open and he spurted, his seed falling to the dirt floor. His body shook as he released his cock and resettled his leather straps. *Forgive my rudeness, seer. I know not what ails me.*

I believe I do. Ariel laughed, then stood before him, saying no more. Eros kissed her on each nipple, then left her quarters.

He had only been able to take the edge off his desire for Rachel momentarily. He'd hoped release would alleviate his need, but if anything he wanted her more. As of this moment he was claimed, no longer allowed to join with another female. He waited to feel a moments discomfort at the thought, but none came.

The time had come to claim his woman.

* * * * *

Rachel awoke with a start. Her giant stood over her holding clothes and a small bowl, his sexy mouth quirked in a lazy smile. His eyes burned like molten lava. Clean blond hair hung past his waist in waves.

She sat up, trying to blink the cobwebs from her sleepy head. His face had been painted in a tribal design similar to those found in Polynesian cultures. She looked out the window. The sky was pitch-black. A few stars were visible where the night breeze blew the leaves apart in the dense treetops. A small fire burned in a kiva, set in the middle of the room.

How long have I been asleep?

"Not long," he answered aloud.

Rachel's jaw dropped. "You speak English." It wasn't a question. He'd shocked her, not only because of the language he used, but because he'd answered her...*thoughts.*

"Do you prefer we converse in another dialect?" He raised a teasing brow.

"No." She stared at those mesmerizing eyes. "English is fine."

"Good."

"What...why...where am I?" Rachel looked around the small hut, as she tried to get her thoughts in order.

Thoughts...he can read my thoughts, all of my thoughts. She grimaced as she recalled exactly where her thoughts had been earlier. "Hey, why didn't you answer me when I tried to talk to you earlier?"

His eyes sparkled with amusement.

"I bet you're getting a real kick out of all this." She waited, but he said nothing, so she continued. "I didn't mean what I was thinking earlier."

"Which thoughts were those?" He put the bowl down on a little table and crossed his arms over his wide chest, the clothes still tightly in his grasp.

Rachel flushed as all the carnal thoughts she'd had involving him rushed back into her mind.

"Oh, those." He smiled, giving her a knowing look. "I rather liked those in particular, especially coming from you."

"I just bet you did, pal." Rachel stood up and put her hands on her hips. Her embarrassment faded into anger. "I want you to take me back to the expedition."

The giant's face closed down, hardening into an unblinking mask. "There will be no returning."

"What exactly do you mean?"

"I mean you shall not leave this place to return to your world."

"What? I have to go back," she shrieked. "You don't understand. I have a life, a job—friends. I can't give that up."

"You don't have a choice."

"You mean you aren't giving me one." Rachel snorted. "I'll escape, you know."

"I don't think so."

"I will the first chance I get." Rachel knew she sounded petulant, but she couldn't help herself.

He shrugged his massive shoulders, as if her threat meant nothing. "I'm here to prepare you for your new position." He picked the bowl back up and began stirring the contents.

"What position is that?"

"You will take your rightful place as our new Queen."

Rachel's jaw dropped as she stared at him, incredulous. "I don't want to be Queen."

"The position is not one of your choosing. Destiny chose long ago." He walked across the small room and picked up a brush from a side storage area that she hadn't noticed earlier.

"What are you planning to do?"

"Prepare you."

"You prepare food, not people."

"Remove your clothes."

Rachel froze. Surely she heard him wrong. He didn't just tell her to take her clothes off. "Now wait just one minute."

"If you don't remove your clothes," he paused, giving her a daring smile, "I'll remove them for you."

He shifted, his muscles flexing and bunching in taut lines. Rachel stared open-mouthed at the giant. She didn't have to read his mind to know he meant what he said, but she refused to be pushed around.

Rachel walked to the bed of furs and plopped down. She put her back against the wall so that she faced him. He stared at her for a few seconds, surprise plainly written on his handsome features. Then a fire sparked in those gemstone depths. He stalked toward her, his gaze never leaving her face.

"You wish to test me?" he growled.

It took every fiber of Rachel's being to keep from fleeing from the blond Adonis. Her heart thudded as he reached the edge of the bed and stopped.

"I'm not taking my clothes off and you can't make me." She hugged her arms around her knees in a protective ball.

The giant reached down, snatched her by the shoulders and pulled her to her feet. Rachel's body exploded into a typhoon of energy. She kicked and screamed, even managing to bite his thick arm before he dropped her back onto the furs. He quickly followed, blanketing her body with his.

Rachel squirmed and squealed to no avail. He pressed her into the bed, his thighs wrapping around her own until she couldn't move at all. She opened her mouth to bite him again and he took the opportunity to plunge his tongue inside, knocking the fight right out of her with a scorching kiss.

His tongue laved at her, teasing, enticing, and inviting her to taste him back. Rachel shuddered. She heard her shirt rip and felt it being pulled away from her body. The sound turned Rachel on more than it should. Something primal came alive within her.

Clinging to his mouth for her next breath, her fingers sought out his sides and she grabbed hold of his slick skin, letting her nails bite deep. He groaned, attacking her ravenously. Rachel surrendered to his sensual assault.

He inserted a knee between her thighs until he'd spread her legs far enough apart to seat himself. Rachel moaned when his rock hard cock came in contact with her clit through the material of her pants. Her hips bucked of their own volition. His teeth nipped at her lower lip, trailing down her jaw and over to her ear.

He bit down on the tender lobe, sending shockwave after shockwave through Rachel's body. She ached with need. Her body responded to his touch as if she'd lain with him a thousand times before.

You have...in your dreams.

He thrust against her and Rachel's channel flooded with her own juices. She had to have this man, right now. She opened her mouth, then closed it, when she realized she was about to beg him to fuck her.

Confused and panicked she pushed him away. "Enough!"

Eros stilled. He'd been so out of his mind with lust that he had almost not heard her plea. What was he doing? This was no way to prepare his woman. Did he want to destroy the only chance his people had for getting off this planet?

Disgusted with his lack of control, he sat up. His body screamed for release, but it would not have it tonight. He stood on shaky legs and held out his hand to Rachel. She placed her fingertips in his and rose.

Her lips were swollen from his kisses and her chocolate colored eyes were glazed. A rosy flush covered much of her skin and her breathing was labored. The shirt she'd been wearing lay in tatters around her shoulders. The scent of her arousal reached out to him, entrancing, enticing, luring. He inhaled and closed his eyes against the temptation.

His voice was graveled as he spoke. "Please, remove your clothes."

Chapter Nine

With trembling fingers she unbuttoned what was left of her outer shirt, pulling it off quickly and dropping it onto the hides. Rachel felt the heat rise in her face as she unzipped her pants. She slipped her T-shirt over her head and toed off her boots. Standing in front of the giant with just her trousers and bra on, she hugged her sides in a futile attempt to cover herself.

"I've seen you bare before." He gave her a slow, sensual smile. "You have nothing to hide, my Queen."

Rachel blushed and waved a hand in the air, dismissing his words. "Yeah well, I didn't know you were there so it kind of changes things."

His smile tuned into a devastating grin. "You were aware of my presence."

"I was n—," Rachel stopped. She *had* known he was there. Maybe not consciously, but subconsciously she'd known it was her dream man lurking in the darkness of the jungle.

"'Tis so, no use denying."

"Okay." She blew out a ragged breath. "But I don't see why I have to remove my clothes." The color drained from her face. "Are you going to rape me?"

The giant looked horrified. "I have never raped a female, and never would I. Your safety is my highest priority. I could never harm you." He ran a frustrated hand through his golden hair. "Women come willingly to my bed furs."

"I just bet they do." She couldn't keep the sarcasm from oozing out in her voice. "Then why do you want me naked?"

Rachel waited, half excited and half terrified by what his answer would be. She tried to ignore the lump that formed in the pit of her stomach at the thought of other women in his bed. It shouldn't bother her one iota, but for some reason it did.

He held up a cloth. "This is the only type of clothing you'll ever need."

Rachel stared at the scrap of material in his outstretched hand. There wasn't enough there to cover one of her thighs, much less anything else.

"You've got to be kidding, Mr...Mr...what is your name?"

"I am known as Eros."

Rachel laughed. She couldn't help herself. "Eros? Like the god of love?" She giggled again and wiped at the tears forming in her eyes.

He can't be serious.

"I'm no god."

"Obviously. Eros is a myth."

He frowned and dropped the clothes at her feet.

"Okay, I'm sorry." She held up her hand in surrender. "It just struck me as funny."

"Put that on." He scowled and pointed to the pile of fabric on the floor.

Obviously he wasn't used to being teased.

Rachel picked up the outfit. The material started to glow everywhere her fingers touched. She ran the sheer garment over her hands and it turned emerald green. It was beautiful. She looked up into Eros's handsome face. He appeared satisfied by her reaction.

"Could you please turn around?"

"We are alone, my Queen. You need not hide yourself from my grateful eyes."

The look Eros gave her appeared almost wounded, as if her asking him to turn hurt him physically, but that wasn't possible. She waited. Finally he faced the door, the pain on his handsome face unmistakable.

Rachel shucked the last of her clothes and tried to put on the outfit he'd brought. She pulled the skirt over her hips, but it kept slipping down, riding low across her pubic bone. She looked around but couldn't find the top.

"Eros, I don't think this is my size."

He swung around and sucked in an audible breath. Rachel covered her breasts with her hands. She felt heat rise over her body as his eyes took in her almost naked form.

"I need the shirt."

"There is no covering for your upper body, as is custom."

"What?" she shouted. "You didn't tell me anything about going topless."

"You didn't ask, my Queen."

"Stop calling me that."

Rachel watched his lips twitch. He thought this whole thing was funny. She shook her head, trying to muster up a look of disgust.

"The skirt's too big," she said between clenched teeth.

"The skirt fits you well, my *Rachel*."

It hardly seemed possible, but hearing her name coming from his mouth struck her with more intimate force than when he had called her "my Queen". Rachel closed her eyes, trying to block out the sexy man before her. He was way too dangerous for her sensibilities.

She tamped down on her feelings, attempting to keep them out of her mind. Rachel gritted her teeth. "It's almost falling off me."

"'Tis as it should be."

Rachel looked down at the loose material. Her pubic hairs stuck out of the top of the skirt it hung so low. The bottom of the drape material reached her ankles. There was no way she was leaving the hut looking like this.

"'Tis the acceptable covering for the women of my tribe."

"Well it may be acceptable for them, but it's not for me. I look like I'm part of a harem."

Eros flashed a grin. "You will get used to it."

"I won't be here long enough to get used to it."

"We aren't finished." Eros raised the brush from the bowl. Red liquid dripped off the end.

"What are you planning to do with th-that...blood?" Rachel's head swam at the thought of having blood spread across her body.

"'Tis dye from the lipstick plant." He swirled the liquid around and around the bowl. "I will paint your nipples with it."

"You'll what?" She backed up, putting distance between them. "You stay away from me, Eros, and keep your kinky tribe away, too."

Eros threw back his head and laughed, vibrating his whole body. He set the paintbrush into the dye. "This will not hurt." He pulled the two gold rings from the side of his loincloth and placed them on the table, then walked to a cabinet that lay hidden in the wall and removed an alien looking instrument that could easily have found a home in a gynecologist office.

"What are you planning on doing with those, and what's that for?" Rachel pointed to the tool in his hand.

She looked from his face to the table where the gold hoops glowed in the firelight, and back to him. A flash of gold on his chest caught her attention. A flutter rose in her belly as her gaze darted from his nipples to the table and back again.

When had he gotten pierced?

Her eyes widened as it fully dawned on her what he wanted to do with the rings. "Oh, no you don't. You're not piercing my nipples." Rachel tried to dodge around him, but tripped on her stupid, pubis-exposing, floor length skirt. She would have fallen face first had Eros not stepped forward, extended his arm and caught her.

"I promise, Queen Rachel, you will not feel pain." His voice grew husky and dropped an octave. "Only pleasure." The words barely left his mouth when Rachel felt her entire body begin to heat from the inside, sending shivery tingles leaping across her skin. He was doing something to her with his hands. She struggled against his firm hold, unable to break the connection.

"Eros, please, no," she whimpered in defeat.

"Trust me."

Rachel fought down the heartache and the overwhelming urge to cry as she remembered another man asking her to trust him. She recalled the agony of finding her fiancé, Stan, in the arms of his bubble-headed blonde secretary, Bambi "boom-boom" Murphy.

Her muscles tensed and she held her breath as Eros raised the first gold hoop to her left nipple, then stopped before he touched her quivering skin. Tears pooled in her eyes and she released a ragged sigh.

Eros lowered his hands and tentatively gripped her arms, his fingertips lightly trailing over her flesh until goosebumps rose. He leaned forward until his forehead touched hers, skin against skin. His breathing, shallow and labored, matched hers breath for breath.

"I am not Stan," he murmured, then rubbed his nose across hers in an Eskimo kiss.

His thumb switched from stroking her arm to gently caressing her nipple, grazing the sensitive nerves with his fingernail, teasing the nub until it tightened and peaked.

Eros dropped to his knees before her and sucked the tip between his lips. He moaned against her breast, licking, nipping, arousing. The rumbling sound only served to enhance her need. He filled his hands with her fullness, devouring her with his insatiable hunger.

Rachel was tired of fighting, tired of trying to resist the carnal demands her body was making on her. Hell, she was tired of being celibate. Men were capable of fucking 'em and forgetting 'em, so why couldn't she be?

With that last fleeting thought, Rachel lost herself in the moment, unable to think or even speak. She relished the feel of Eros feeding at her ample bosom. Her head dropped back, exposing the long column of her neck. She moaned, sinking her trembling fingers into Eros's blond locks. He was satin and fire all rolled up into one and she couldn't get enough.

Eros guided the hoop in place. A quick pop and Rachel's left nipple was pierced.

Rachel jumped, her unfocused gaze latching upon the gold hoop now dangling from her areola. She'd all but forgotten what his original intention had been. As promised, she didn't feel a thing.

Eros smiled. He knew his eyes were as glazed over as hers. He stuck out his tongue. Only then did he see surprise register on Rachel's flushed face. Eros watched emotion flash in her eyes as memories from that night in her tent flooded her mind. Her right nipple beaded instantly.

He swirled his tongue around the kernelled bead a couple times, refusing to break eye contact with Rachel. Her breathing deepened and she closed her eyes. Eros took that moment to finish the piercing. It was done. She was officially claimed in the eyes of the Atlantean people. He stood. The heat flowing from his hands intensified and the wounds healed before his eyes, along with cleansing her body of the dirt and sweat that had accumulated.

Rachel looked up into his face, stunned, unable to move. Never in her life could she imagine being pierced anywhere but her ears. The rings made her feel sexy, dangerous and more than a little naughty. She watched Eros pick up the bowl and raise the paintbrush to each nipple, leaving red dye in its place.

The bristles stroked and tickled. Eros swished the brush back and forth and an answering wetness formed between her legs.

She swallowed hard. Heaven help her, she was getting so turned on. In another minute or two, she'd end up attacking him if he didn't stop.

Eros dropped the brush into the dye and pulled his knife from its sheath. He raised the blade to Rachel's waist, then lowered the knife to her pubic bone.

"Uh uh. No way. Not a chance." Rachel backed away with her hands held out to prevent Eros's next move. "It's one thing to pierce my nipples, but there's no way in hell I'm letting you near my clit. So you can forget about it."

Eros laughed heartily. The deep rumbling sound washed over her like the spray from a waterfall. His eyes sparkled with mirth. He wiped his hand across his face, apparently trying to hide his amused smile.

"The blade is not for piercing, 'tis for shaving."

Rachel's body throbbed with need. Just the thought of his hands on her, shaving her bare was enough to almost send her over the edge. The intimacy of the act was on par with a man painting her toenails, although she'd yet to experience that either. She felt like a mass of electrified nerve endings, reaching out to make contact with the one being that could ground them. The rings on her nipples felt cool against her heated skin.

He closed the distance between them and carefully brought the blade to her mound. With precision, he began to shave her pubic hair off.

With the first scrape of the cool steel across her sensitive skin, Rachel's pussy lips became drenched in her own juices. Each stroke of the razor's sharp edge was erotic, intoxicating—intimate. Her clit began to swell and pulse, until Rachel was incapable of anything more than animalistic moans.

Eros sliced over her tuft-covered skin once more and Rachel's knees buckled. He held her firm in his arms, pressing her into his side until he'd completed his task. He sheathed his knife and lifted up a corner of her skirt, sliding one hand beneath, scraping his short nails across her hip.

Rachel shuddered. Her body felt as if it would fly apart in a million pieces. Eros placed his hand upon her abdomen. The same intense heat that she'd felt earlier seemed to concentrate its energy on her womb, then lower still. Her body convulsed, as an orgasm hit that literally knocked her off her feet.

Eros sat on the floor and pulled Rachel onto his lap. He ran a fingertip along her slit. Wetness covered him as he sought out her pleasure center. He massaged his way up and down her outer lips, teasing her, drawing out her satisfaction. One finger slipped inside her tight opening. She felt like heaven on Earth.

His cock throbbed and pulsed under the loincloth. He grit his teeth and continued finger fucking her. Rachel's eyes closed and her body trembled. He pulled his wet finger out and circled her clit. She moaned. He looped around and around until her breath came out in panting gasps.

Her body's tremors started once more from deep inside and radiated out. He kept up the lazy motions, leaning down to cover her mouth with his, hungry, wanting, and needing much more.

Eros captured her scream as Rachel came once again. He kissed her deeply, pulling her into his chest, probing the recesses of her mouth with his seeking tongue. She tasted of the sweetest honey, the tangiest nectar, and she was his…all his.

Rachel's body swayed with the force of her second orgasm. Eros had promised her pleasure and he'd delivered. His kisses were heated with a passion beyond her comprehension.

Eros, the god of love.

What was she doing? She pushed against his muscled chest, trying to free herself from his lap. She had to get away from this godlike man before she did something stupid, like agree to stay. Rachel shoved again.

He broke the kiss reluctantly and allowed her to pull away. His eyes were glazed and his hard-on was enormous. Rachel felt an instant pang of regret. She missed the warmth of being held in his arms. The comfort of his touch.

She didn't need this. She didn't need him. She had a life, an apartment—a job waiting for her back in New York. It'd be for the best if she tried to remember that. Jac and Brigit were probably worried sick.

And why in the hell did I let him pierce my nipples?

Rachel stood and took a step back, hoping that the little space would afford her more breathing room and better sense. "Thanks, but I don't want you getting the idea that I'm easy, just because I let you…let you…"

"Pleasure you?" He raised a wicked eyebrow.

"Why did you," she paused searching for the right words, "do all this?"

"To prepare you for the mating ceremony."

She could not have heard him right. "For what?"

"You heard me, Rachel."

Rachel pushed her hair away from her face and began nervously twisting the strands into a bun. She always wore her hair up when she had a serious meeting at work to attend. It made her feel confident, professional—and she needed all those traits now.

She blew out an unsteady breath. "I heard you. I just don't believe you. There really must be some mistake. I'm no Queen. I'm not a Princess. I'm not even a native New Yorker." Rachel dropped her hair and began kneading her palms. "I'm just plain ol' Dr. Rachel Evans from Salem, Massachusetts."

Eros followed her with his eyes, patiently listening to all her reasons of denial. "That was your old existence," he said, folding his arms over his broad chest. "Here you are Queen to the people of Atlantis."

"Sure." She smiled in a let's-soothe-the-man-who-forgot-to-take-his-medication-way. "I'm Queen," she pointed to herself, "and you're from the fabled city of Atlantis." She shook her head and began to pace. A nervous giggle escaped her throat. "Just my luck, I meet a gorgeous guy and he's crazy."

"You know I speak the truth. You've witnessed my powers."

"I realize you believe that what you're saying to me is the truth." She stopped and raised her hands. "But it's crazy, not to mention impossible, since Atlantis has never been proven to exist. Besides at this moment, I'm convinced I definitely have malaria or some other fever-inducing malady. I'm not sure if anything I'm seeing is real."

"You will understand soon," he smiled, "once the mating ceremony is complete and my seed is planted deep within your womb." Eros began clearing the dye and brush off the table. He returned them to the compartment hidden in the side of the wall. Rachel glimpsed tools and other instruments, before he stepped away, closing the case behind him.

Now is not the time for curiosity, she mentally chastised. *I've got more important things to take care of here.*

Rachel faced Eros, her fingers resting lightly on her hips. "There isn't going to be a mating ceremony or planting of seed. I'm not a farmer's field. Where I'm from people don't usually mate to have babies, unless they're married. And seeing as though we're not wed, this conversation is mute." She reddened. It made her uncomfortable to discuss this with him.

"Exactly."

"Ooogh, are you trying to piss me off?" Rachel balled her hands into tight fists, but resisted the urge to slug the jerk. She figured if she hit him, the only person who'd get hurt would be her. Besides, he was mentally unstable. She should humor him.

Eros stepped forward, raising his hands to take her in his arms, but stopped short. "I'm not trying to upset you, my Queen, although I seem to be successful in that respect." The corners of his firm lips quirked in a half smile. "I speak the truth."

Rachel reached out and covered his mouth with her hand, trying to quiet him long enough for her to think things through. He kissed her palm, flicking his tongue at its center.

She quickly pulled away and tried to regain her composure. The skin still tingled where his lips had touched. "Okay, let's say for the sake of argument that I'm Queen, then who is King?"

Eros smiled slowly, an erotically carnal action that caused the proverbial curling of her toes. "I am." He kissed her forehead, turned, and walked out of the hut.

Chapter Ten

A queer sensation twisted in Rachel's belly, and she was rendered speechless. Confusing emotions and thoughts swirled through her, all fighting one another for attention.

He'd said she'd been chosen by this tribe to mate with him, but that was ridiculous. She wished that the thought of having sex with him was unappealing, but ever since she'd laid eyes on him, saying that would have been a bald-faced lie.

If she'd met Eros in New York she'd probably have thrown herself at him and begged the big oaf to fuck her silly, until she couldn't walk the next day. And that was saying a lot coming from a girl that had been celibate for the last two years.

She looked down at her nipples, bright red with dye, complete with glittering gold rings. Considering what a god Eros was, she'd probably have let him pierce her in New York, too. Hell, she'd probably have allowed him to tattoo his name across her forehead.

Rachel rolled her eyes as her thoughts turned to Eros and his people, their beauty almost astonishing in its perfection. Rachel glanced down at her body. She wasn't even going to go there right now. These people seemed to have developed a form of telepathic language that would leave even the top psychics envious. Not that Rachel believed in those kinds of abilities, but it was hard to ignore what she'd seen. That left, of course, Eros's ability to generate healing energy from his hands. Was it real? Rachel sighed. She wasn't sure of anything anymore.

What if the lost civilization of Atlantis existed and ended up on the other side of the world? Not that she lent the thought any credence.

So many theories existed about Atlanteans. One popular hypothesis was that it had sunk due to a volcanic eruption equivalent to the disaster in Pompeii. Another researcher found what he thought was proof of a giant tidal wave. Yet another believed Atlanteans originated from the area of the Bermuda Triangle.

The most radical of the bunch of theorists was a professor of ancient civilizations. His hypothesis stated that Atlanteans developed a society so advanced that their technological expertise destroyed them.

Rachel decided that once she returned to the museum she'd dedicate some time to reading the research papers that had been written on the subject.

If these people were Atlanteans, this would be the discovery of a lifetime.

Society could benefit from their knowledge. Rachel would be recognized in all the anthropological journals, receive book deals, do the talk show circuit—the sky was the limit. Professor Donald could then slither back under the rock from which he came.

She had to think of a way out of here. Maybe if she left tonight she'd be able to get out of the tree without her fear of heights kicking in. It would be dark, so she wouldn't see the steep drop. Rachel swallowed the burst of fear and reaffirmed her decision. She would wait until the tribe had gone to sleep, then she would make her escape.

Rachel wondered where Eros had gone. Would he be sleeping with one of his many women tonight? The thought chafed her ass. He'd better not be fucking someone else, not if he expected to become her mate.

What am I saying?

There will be no mating ceremony, no coronation – no nothing. I'm out of here in a couple of hours. What Eros does is no concern of mine.

Hours passed and the village quieted. Rachel threw back the hide covering the door and peeked out. Fear and panic gripped at her insides like a living entity trying to pull her back inside. No one stirred in the surrounding huts. The moon would be full by tomorrow night, so it would be fairly easy to find her way out of the encampment.

Eros was nowhere to be seen.

He's probably in bed with some slut. She ignored the pain that came with that thought.

Rachel walked back into the hut, donned her pants and T-shirt and retrieved her cell phone. She pocketed the phone, reluctantly dropped the beautiful skirt on the hides and headed out the door. Her nipple rings felt strange against her bra.

Talk about your souvenirs.

Before leaving, she tucked the tool Eros had used to pierce her inside one of her pockets. She now had the necessary evidence to prove that she'd actually been in an Atlantean society, or at the very least around a previously undiscovered tribe.

The moon cast ominous shadows on the jungle floor. Walking along the outside of the hut, she kept her back against the wall until she reached the corner of the building. Several vines hung from the trees in a mess of tangles. Rachel fought back the queasiness that threatened to empty her stomach's contents.

It's now or never.

Rachel reached out and grabbed a vine, pulling on it firmly to ensure the rope like growth would hold her weight. She looked over her shoulder once more, but there was no movement.

She blew out a steadying breath. *Exactly like gym class. Just don't look down.*

Stifling a scream, Rachel swung onto the vine and slid down as silently as possible. The rope slithered between her thighs, rubbing her clit through her pants. The gold rings on her nipples brushed her T-shirt, sending erotic sensations coursing through her body. She clamped her lips together to keep from groaning.

Rachel's booted feet hit the ground. She released the breath she hadn't known she'd been holding. Rachel let go of the vine and pushed her body against the tree. There was still no sign of any disturbance. A voice niggled at the back of her mind, *this is too easy*, but she ignored it.

She searched the night sky until she located the North Star. She did a few quick calculations in her mind of the time she'd need to reach the river. She paused just long enough to get her bearings.

Ready, set – go.

Rachel took off running as fast as she could. Vines and undergrowth snarled at her feet, but didn't slow her pace. She snapped branches and crushed ferns, running as hard as she could, always with one ear listening to see if someone followed. Her breathing was ragged and her legs burned.

After fifteen minutes of hard running, she slowed to a clipped jog. She'd lost sight of the North Star and had no idea what direction she was heading. Rachel prayed she wasn't running in circles and that the river would appear in a few hours. If she got really lucky she'd run into the Professor.

And then I can kill him.

After she enjoyed the shock on his face at seeing her return from the dead. Rachel knew she was talking nonsense. She couldn't kill anything, but it made her feel better to think it. The best she could hope for was stumbling across her pack and retrieving Jac's present or getting the jump on one of the smaller guides and taking his gun from him.

Two hours later, out of breath and out of steam, Rachel walked until she couldn't take another step.

What was she going to do? She still hadn't found a sign of water or her pack. She dropped to her knees next to a large tree that had partially eroded away. The arc shaped nook would provide adequate shelter for the night, and hopefully a hiding place if Eros came looking. Rachel rested her back against the bark and closed her eyes. She'd done it. She'd escaped. Unfortunately, the thought did not bring her any solace.

* * * * *

Eros fought the urge to swoop down and retrieve his woman. She'd led him on a merry chase through the jungle tonight. The pain of her rejection tore at his insides. He blew out a heavy breath. In time she'd learn to love him as much as he already loved her and if not, well he'd learn to live with it.

For now he'd have to be content in the tree above her, watching her sleep. His chest contracted, as if he'd received a physical blow. Tonight he'd let her feel a small moment of victory. Tomorrow he'd collect her and return her to the village.

In the end, she would not win.

A bitter hollow victory for him since the decision would not be of her choosing.

He was about to nod off when the crunching sound of movement caught his attention. Several members of Rachel's expedition were making their way through the jungle, heading straight toward Rachel's hiding place.

Eros unsheathed his knife. There were many, but he'd kill every last one of the men before he'd let them take his woman.

* * * * *

Rachel woke with a start. She'd heard something, but in her dreamlike state she wasn't sure what. She listened.

There it was again.

Someone was coming.

Panic struck. She pushed her body against the tree and stilled her breathing. She hadn't come this far, only to have freedom ripped away from her. The noise drew nearer. Rachel recognized a couple of the voices. It was the expedition. Torn by fear and indecision, she stayed in place.

What would the men do once they discover I'm alive? Kill me?

She could stay rooted against the tree or take the chance that they'd be too scared to do anything other than, very worse case scenario, return her to the Professor. Hopefully in the time it took to get to Donald, she'd be able to acquire a weapon. Rachel decided to take her chances with her first captors, even though her heart sank at the thought of leaving her giant behind.

For a moment she pictured Eros, his beautiful body all lean and strong, standing proud in the doorway of his hut. His gaze burning with fire as he lovingly caressed her. Rachel took a ragged breath. She'd miss her giant.

Would she ever see his handsome face again, or taste his passionate kisses? Would he forgive her for leaving him if she did return one day? Rachel doubted he'd welcome her back with open arms, his pride would not allow it.

Rachel jumped out of the crevice, knowing there would be no happily ever after for them. She listened for the men, then followed their footsteps like a bloodhound. She was about to round the next tree when she tripped. Rachel felt around on the ground trying to figure out what the obstruction was when her hands encountered a pack. It wouldn't be, could it? Her heart leapt for joy as her fingers dove to the bottom, encountering Jac's little present. Relief flooded her as she rose to her feet, tucked the Glock against the small of her back and raced forward to catch up with the group. She came upon the men in less than five minutes.

Rachel let out a bloodcurdling scream followed by a loud, "Boo!"

The guides were swinging the beams of their flashlights wildly about, making the jungle look like a rave party. Their eyes were wide with fear and surprise. She didn't see Jaro, but did recognize the other men. There was a lot of pushing and shoving along with frantic shouts about her being a ghost. The scene was utter chaos.

Afraid of angering the dead, not a single man reached for his gun. She had to hide a giggle at that. Let them think she'd returned from the dead. It would serve them right. The fear would actually work to her advantage.

Rachel raised her arms above her head, waggling her fingers menacingly. "Take me to the Professor or I will snatch your souls while you sleep," she shouted in their native tongue.

Wild eyes looked from her to the jungle and back again. Some of the men were praying, while others begged her forgiveness. Rachel just leered and pointed at each man as if determining which one to take. The men quivered and shook. Several guides jumped up and ran off, disappearing in the thick undergrowth.

Donald pushed his way through the crowd and appeared at the front of the group. His face twisted in fury the moment he saw Rachel. "What are you doing here, Evans? You're supposed to be dead."

"I didn't like being dead, so I came back. I have some unfinished business to settle." Rachel fought to control the fear racing through her veins. The Professor would jump on any sign of weakness.

"What would that be, Dr. Evans?" His tone was deceptively cool.

"I need to get the asshole fired that left me here to die in the jungle and, with any luck, arrested for attempted murder."

Donald's cheek twitched. "I'm not a fool like these idiots," he spat out as he waved a hand aggressively at the guides. "If you're dead, then so am I."

Rachel laughed. "Not yet, you're not."

The flashlight Donald held gave him a freakish yellow overtone. His knuckles were white from the pressure he applied to the handle. He clenched his jaw, gnashing his teeth together like a rabid dog. His eyes burned with unchecked fury.

Rachel put her hands on her hips and glared at him.

"What's the matter, Professor? Cat got your tongue?"

Donald stilled. His features went flat until there was no emotion visible. Rachel knew better than to poke a snake with a stick, but she continued to goad the Professor anyhow. She no longer owed him anything. His gaze zeroed in on her, pinning her in place. The hatred she saw in those depths frightened her.

Rachel swallowed hard. Maybe she hadn't thought this plan through well enough. She stood her ground, even though every fiber of her being screamed at her to run. The air pressed in around them. She fumbled for the gun at her back, unable to grasp the handle in time.

In a flash he drew a weapon from its holster. Rachel found herself staring down the barrel of a pistol in disbelief. *Her own pistol, the one the Professor had found down by the water.* Donald shouted to the men to vacate the area, and in seconds she and the Professor were alone.

The air rushed from her lungs, muscles in her chest constricted so tight she feared they'd stop her heart from beating. Rachel took another step back. Donald meant to kill her without witnesses. She raised her hands as if to surrender, praying that the Professor would get distracted long enough for her to be able to reach and pull the gun from the small of her back.

"All I want to do is get back home to New York," she sputtered and choked. "Can't we work something out?"

"It's too late for that, Dr. Evans."

Rachel's fingers trembled as she pointed to the gun in his hand. "It's never too late, as long as you don't pull that trigger."

"Oh, but it is. You see I have no plans to go to jail."

"What about the men?"

"They will have to meet with a tragic demise. Accidents occur everyday in the jungle. Such is life." He wagged the gun in the air. "Perhaps I'll tell the authorities you went crazy and shot several of the guides."

"You're going to kill every one of them?" Rachel shook her head in denial. "You're mad." She put her hands in front of her, as if that would block the oncoming bullet.

"Maybe so, but you're still going to die. The beauty of it is, and I'm sure you'll agree, I will use your gun." Donald licked his chapped lips as if salivating at the prospect of killing her.

"But I...I've made an incredible discovery." Rachel dropped one hand to the pocket that held the piercing instrument.

His brow arched. "What *kind* of discovery?" His gaze followed her movements, giving Rachel no opportunity to reach her weapon.

She lowered her other hand, once she realized he'd taken the bait. She rubbed her palms along her pants, trying to wipe away some of the nervous perspiration. "Like the leaf, but better. This one will make us famous."

Donald kept the pistol pointed at her, but Rachel could see curiosity sparking in his eyes. He was weighing her words, trying to figure out if she was bluffing. Finally he lowered the weapon.

I should just take the instrument out and show him.

"What have you discovered?" The gun was still in his hand, he hadn't bothered returning it to its holster. "This better be good Doctor. Your life depends on it." He shook the barrel at her, gesturing for her to continue.

Rachel stomach turned. She wondered what would become of Eros once the Professor reached the village. She didn't want Donald destroying her discovery, but at the same time, this was the only card left she could play to save her own life.

Hopefully Eros would understand. Rachel knew her giant wouldn't stand idly by and let the outside world intrude on his people. He'd go down fighting.

Rachel swallowed hard, trying to get the lump forming in her throat to disappear. She blinked back tears. It didn't bear thinking about. Rachel couldn't go through with this. She couldn't do that to Eros...

She *loved* him. Rachel thought of the dreams she'd had while in New York. *Maybe I always have.* With that revelation came a deeper understanding. She'd never give up Eros's people. She'd die first.

"Nothing!" Rachel couldn't believe the word had left her mouth. But there it was floating in the air between them. She moved her hands away from her pockets.

"Nothing?" he raged.

"I found nothing," she ground out, with a fierce determination she hadn't known existed within her.

Rachel would rather die than see the Professor lay his grubby hands on Eros's people.

Donald raised the gun and leveled the sites. Rachel closed her eyes, not wanting to see the bullet coming, but opened them quickly when she heard the Professor chuckle. The night quieted, stifled by the tension crackling between them.

Defiant, Rachel focused on the Professor. Bile rose up in her throat as she realized he would be the last sight she'd see before meeting her death. She closed her eyes again and pictured Eros.

Donald cocked the gun and fired. The *kaboom* sound seemed far away in Rachel's mind, like a distant crack of thunder heralding a storm. Her eyes flew open and she braced, waiting for the bullet's impact. Yet she felt no pain. Had he missed? Rachel wasn't going to wait to find out. Her hand automatically reached for the Glock. With trembling fingers she pulled it free and aimed at the Professor. One minute Donald stood before her, the next he was rolling on the ground holding his head. Had she fired? She didn't remember pulling the trigger. Her limbs were trembling so badly she wasn't sure.

In the next instant, the gun was wrenched from her hands and the jungle floor was gone. Rachel found herself swooped up and flying through the air, wrapped in a pair of strong arms, against a warm muscled body.

Eros...

Rachel looked down then squeezed her lids shut.

"Look at me." The request came as a calm whisper amidst the turmoil.

She dared to open her eyes. Eros looked into her face, his fear for her plainly written across his chiseled features.

Tears sprang to her eyes. He squeezed her tighter. He smelled woodsy and fresh.

"Is he dead?"

His jaw clenched. "No. The blow I sent him was only enough to keep him from killing you. It happened too fast for my aim to be lethal." His arm tightened around her.

Rachel shuddered. She hadn't meant to frighten him. She just wanted to go home.

Why did it have to feel so right being in his arms?

She held him tight around his waist as he caught lianas vine after vine. The speed at which they were moving was blinding. They reached the village in record time. He swung up in front of his hut door, his feet making no sound on the tree limb. He pushed aside the hide and stepped over the threshold without releasing her.

Eros walked over to the furs on the floor and carefully laid Rachel upon them. With trembling fingers, he brushed back her hair, his touch gentle as he examined her. His face glowed with a warmth and tenderness that made Rachel's heart ache.

He loved her, too.

The stunning realization scared Rachel spitless.

What was she going to do? She couldn't stay here, *could she?*

No, no definitely not. She had an apartment back in New York.

You've got one room, the little voice said.

She had her job.

Not when the Professor gets done with his smear campaign. Hell, that's if he let's me live long enough to see the museum again.

Friends. She'd miss Jac and Brigit.

She had to go back, if only to see those she loved again. Her eyes were drawn to a streak of red on Eros's arm. He'd been shot. The bullet meant for her had struck him.

Rachel's stomach dropped. "Oh, my god. Are you all right?" She grabbed the remnants of her tattered shirt and dabbed at the wound.

Eros stilled her hand, his eyes meeting hers. "I'm well, my Queen." His hand began to glow and the injury disappeared.

"H-How?"

"Sleep, one whose mind is active like the monkeys. We'll discuss it tomorrow," Eros murmured, his voice low and soothing. "You showed braveness tonight worthy of a Queen." He stripped his loincloth off and stood before Rachel as naked as the day he came into this world.

Magnificent, was the only word that came to mind as she gazed upon him at length. He leaned over and removed her outfit, like a patient father getting a child ready for bed. Soon they were both naked.

Rachel held her breath, but he didn't make a move. For a moment, she felt disappointed. *Why hadn't he tried anything?*

Eros lowered his body onto the furs beside her and covered his eyes with his arms. She turned on her side to look upon him. Deep lines were etched in his face from worry and exhaustion. He smelled musky and sweet, sexy and hot, devastatingly male.

Soon his breathing deepened and Rachel realized he'd fallen asleep. She listened for several minutes to the sound of his breathing, barely able to keep her eyes open. There was something about the man that made her insides squishy, made her consider childish things like fairytales and happy endings.

Would they have a happy ending? Was there really such a thing?

Not likely.

Sooner or later reality always set in. One or more of the people in a relationship got bored and strayed. That was just the way it was in the real world.

"Rest, my Queen. Ponder our future in the morning." His voice sleepy, but strong, lulled her into a comfortable slumber.

Chapter Eleven

Rachel woke, curled into warmth that equaled a furnace. She snuggled closer, her butt finding a perfect fit against a hard, throbbing cock. Rachel's eyes flew open and she froze, afraid to move a muscle. The thick rod pulsed against her ass. Eros had one arm thrown over her, holding her body in place, and his thigh had somehow managed to weave its way between her legs.

He shifted and his muscled thigh brushed her clit, sending tingles spiraling over her skin like a thousand tiny butterflies caressing her. Rachel shuddered. Her body came alive instantly. She bit down on her lip to keep from moaning aloud. Eros moved again, this time slightly up and across. Her breathing caught and her pussy drenched.

"I see you're awake, my Queen," he purred. His penetrating baritone seeped over her, going straight to her quivering nipples.

Rachel blushed. Fighting her body's need she tried to pull away from him to no avail. It was like trying to escape a vise.

"Do you not wish me to pleasure you?" The promise his voice held set her blood on fire.

"I...a..." Rachel's mind refused to function. Eros had raised his leg higher. Her pussy now fully rode his thigh. She groaned, closing her eyes.

"I thought so."

Rachel knew without looking that he had a smug smile planted on his face.

He started a slow pulse up and down. He placed his hands upon her hips and moved her back and forth at the same time. The sensation was pure torture. Rachel threw her hips back and clamped her legs tighter around his thigh, riding in reckless abandon. Pressure built inside her, fanning out. Her pussy throbbed as it made contact with taut muscles. He firmly pressed her down, grinding her clit.

Rachel's orgasm hit strong, knocking the breath from her lungs.

Trembling, she collapsed back against Eros's broad chest. He slid his fingers around to play in her wetness, then stroked up until he reached her pierced nipples. He stuck a finger in each loop and pulled ever so slightly, the sensation sending another shudder through her.

Eros lifted her off his leg and gently laid her on her back. He pressed his body to hers, nipple-to-nipple, thigh-to-thigh, cunt-to-cock. His eyes locked with Rachel's, as if waiting to see if she'd accept him.

Rachel exploded with need. She wanted Eros inside her now. Buried to the hilt. Fucking her mindless. Her hips rotated in encouragement, tilting her wet channel to ease his entrance. He stilled her movements. "Soon," he muttered before capturing her mouth in a heated kiss. His lips explored hers, nibbling and caressing. His tongue plunged then retreated.

Eros broke the embrace. He clenched his jaw and dropped his head forward until his forehead rested upon Rachel's. Sweat beaded his brow and the lines on his face looked strained. He closed his eyes and thrust against her once, his breath coming in warm pants against her cheek. Rachel felt the slide of the satiny hardness against her pussy. Her mind locked, refusing to function. She needed this man inside her now. Eros slid down her body quickly as if to avoid further temptation. Rachel groaned. He spread her thighs apart with his broad shoulders, opening her wide. She glanced down. Her pussy lips were swollen and engorged. The sight of him between her legs was beyond erotic. Her breath caught in her lungs, as he rolled his tongue seductively.

Eros plunged into her cunt with his serpent-like tongue, lapping at her, swirling around, repeatedly driving in deeper and deeper, until her body convulsed with a second blinding orgasm. Rachel sunk her fingers into his silky hair, drawing him nearer.

Rachel screamed, her body all but jackknifing off the bed. Her thighs clamped around his head. Her mind shattered into a billion fragments of light. Never in her life had she ever experienced this level of pleasure. Her pussy pulsed and throbbed. Her skin flushed, while her nipples stabbed skyward. She could feel the ripples vibrating out, spilling through her senses as wave after wave rocked her.

Only with Eros.

Eros licked Rachel's juices from his chin, like a hungry predator savoring his prey. She tasted sweet and tangy, like the camu camu fruit. Her musk surrounded him, drowning his senses. He could easily feed on her pussy for an eternity. His cock ached from staving off his orgasm. One more day to go and the mating ceremony would take place. He hoped by tomorrow he'd be able to convince her to accept him in her heart, as well as her bed. Her verbal proclamation of love remained essential to a successful union.

He'd already claimed her. Once they were joined, he'd never let her go.

Rachel showed signs of trust whether she knew it or not. The way she snuggled against him in her sleep, the way she looked at him, her gaze filled with longing. She allowed him to touch her any way he desired.

She had even trusted him not to drop her as they swung through the trees last night, despite the fact that heights terrified her. It had killed Eros to wait as the Professor aimed the gun at Rachel, but for his own peace of mind, he had to see if she would remain loyal to him and the people of Atlantis.

Little by little her resistance was wearing down.

Soon she'd love him, as much as his heart loved her.

Today he would show Rachel the village and introduce her to his people. Perhaps if he explained to her the significance of her being here, she'd understand and want to stay. The seer might be able to help. He'd take Rachel to talk to her this afternoon. For now, he just wanted to enjoy the taste of her on his lips. Explore her curves, until he had them memorized. Record her sensuous moans in his mind.

Eros rose from the furs. He held his hand out to help Rachel up. She rose onto her knees, tugging her hand free from his grasp. Her brown eyes sparked with sensuality and her pink tongue darted out to wet her bottom lip. Eros narrowed his gaze.

What was she up to now?

He was about to ask when she slipped her small hands around the base of his cock. "By the goddess, what are you doing?" he bit out, his voice strained from the effort.

She arched a delicate brow in challenge. "You want me to stop?"

"No!" he bellowed. He'd dreamt about the feel of her small hands upon him, he didn't want her to stop now.

"I didn't think so." She laughed, the sound rich and pleasing to his ears. The sparkle in her eyes disappeared, replaced by burning desire in its stead, as she gazed longingly upon his staff.

"I've wanted to do this ever since I met you in my dream." With that she licked the underside of his cock from end to end.

Eros blew out a heavy breath. He wasn't sure what dream she talked about, but if she wanted to touch him, he would not protest. His gaze dropped to her full lips as she sucked the crown of his cock into her mouth. Her fingers took on an intoxicating rhythm, sliding seductively around his girth. Eros was so busy watching her hands that his knees almost buckled when she took him to the back of her throat. Her mouth could barely accept a portion of his length, but it was enough. Warmth surrounded him, enveloping, firing off every instinct to claim and conquer. His cock was cradled while she suctioned the very life from his body.

His palms sought out her head. Eros rested his fingertips in her silky hair, following her bobbing movements. She suckled and licked, swirling her tongue around his cock, playing with the eye. The moist lashing drove all rational thought from his mind. He tried to focus on her goddess-like face, but his vision began to blur. His need rose like an inferno, searing his blood.

Eros labored for every breath, trying to draw out the pleasure she gifted him with. His legs shook and his body trembled. A thin sheen of sweat covered his golden skin as he tried to hang on. His grip tightened of its own accord. He was a warrior damn it, a King. He should last longer than a mere squire...but her lips were wreaking havoc on his good intentions. His shaft strained to gain deeper entrance, seeking the heaven-like release her ministrations would bring.

Rachel sucked in hard and it was all over. Eros thrust in her mouth, unable to stop himself. He felt his heavy sac rise up against his cock, pulling the rest of him over a precipice.

He jerked, his seed squirted forth, flowing out of his body, spilling down Rachel's throat. He tried to pull back, but she held him firmly, gripping his buttocks with one hand, his cock with the other, as she swallowed every drop. Eros thrust a couple more times against her mouth, his loins aflame.

Rachel ran her tongue along his length once more, catching the last few pearly drops easing from his body, and sat back on her heels. A "cat licking cream from its whiskers" smile spread across her face, warming his soul.

Eros dropped to his knees before her. His eyes locked to hers. His breathing still hadn't returned to normal. "You are truly a sorceress."

He brought his mouth to hers, kissing her hard, tasting his own essence on her lips, then dropped his head to place a quick peck upon each of her nipples, resisting the urge to suckle, before rising.

Eros carefully pulled her off the furs as if she were fragile. He dressed her in the traditional outfit and then slipped his loincloth on.

Food had already been set outside the door, as was the custom during the preparation period. He lifted the hide blocking the door and grabbed the bowl of fruits and fresh bread.

"Let us take nourishment. You have much to see today." Eros set the food upon the table. They sat and ate companionably.

Rachel shared the adventures in shopping that she had with her friends Jac and Brigit. She talked of parties and luncheons, even holidays. The love she had for the two women was apparent. She choked up while talking about them, pretending that a piece of fruit got lodged in her throat.

Eros didn't question her, but felt guilty that he'd caused her pain.

Rachel shared her ambitions with him and explained to Eros in great detail what her field of study in school had been.

Eros listened intently, hanging on her every word. Gripping the table, he hesitated, then asked. "Can you interpret symbols?"

"What kind of symbols?" Rachel mumbled over the bite of banana she'd taken.

Eros sat back. He knew in order to gain trust, first you must give it. He looked at his future mate. Her hair lay in disarray from their earlier frolic. It was time to trust her with more than his heart.

"We have a transport here that no one has been able to interpret since the sages were lost. Would you be interested in seeing it?"

"Transport? You mean like a ship?" Rachel's eye lit up with excitement. "I'd love to." She took another bite of banana. Her gaze fixed on the discarded peel, obviously lost in thought.

Eros picked up pictures of flying discs, gray aliens, Roswell, and strewn wreckage from her scattered thoughts. None of the images made any sense to him.

Slowly she raised her eyes to meet his. "What happened to the sages?"

"Some were killed, some escaped to Zaron, our home planet." The ache of loss flooded Eros. Over two thousand years had passed since the great disaster, yet the pain felt fresh every time he spoke of Atlantis.

"Did you say planet?" She held up her hand. "No, don't tell me, I don't want to know."

He nodded and watched as her brows furrowed. After a few seconds she frowned, her disbelief as transparent as her emotions. When she changed the subject, he decided not to push the point.

"What about your parents?"

"Lost..." Eros looked away from Rachel. He didn't want to see pity on her face. He wanted only her understanding, her love.

Rachel cleared her throat. "How old were you when they died?"

"I was thirteen of your years."

"I'm sorry," she gulped. "My folks are dead, too."

He turned back to prevent her from saying any more, but stopped as her words registered. Tears pooled in her brown eyes, covering her lashes, a moment before they spilled down her pale cheeks.

Eros reached out and captured some of the wetness on his fingertips. He leaned across the table and placed a kiss on each cheek, feeling the salt upon his lips. Pulling back to frame her face with his large palms, he tilted her chin up until their eyes met.

"Please don't cry, *my* Rachel. We have each other." He brought his mouth to hers in a tender kiss before releasing her.

"It's just so sad." Rachel swiped at the fresh tears with the back of her hand. "I don't know what I would have done if I'd lost my parents when I was growing up. It was bad enough losing them at twenty-one. If it weren't for my friends, Jac and Brigit, I'd be all alone in this world. They are my family now."

Eros's eyes flashed at her words, but he said nothing.

Eros had experienced the worst kind of loss as a child. Rachel tried to imagine him as a boy. His hair golden, those aquamarine eyes flashing with mischief. He was probably a handful for his mother and father. She wondered which one he most resembled. The truth was, she'd never know.

She frowned. "You were so young."

"I was not the only one who lost loved ones that day. Many have suffered." Eros's jaw tightened and he crushed the piece of fruit he'd just pick up from the table. "Their only hope was that the seer's prophecy of your arrival, our impending union and ultimately the conception of our child, would prove true."

Rachel blew out a ragged breath. "Prophecy? Baby? This is too much. How do you expect me to believe all this? Eros, I can't even believe I'm the one chosen to save your people. Look at me." She stood and twirled around in a circle. "I'm an average woman, in every sense of the word. There is nothing special about me." She stopped and faced him. "And motherhood? I'm not ready to be a mother." *Was she?*

Eros flinched as she uttered her last words, but continued on. "Ah, but that's where you are wrong, my Rachel. There is nothing average about you." A knowing smile curled his lips. "When the red-haired demon was about to end your life you had the chance to save yourself by telling him where to find my people, and showing him the instrument in your pocket, yet you chose to remain silent. You were brave and loyal, like a Queen should be."

"That's different." *Wasn't it?*

"No, 'tis not. You have told me about your friendship with Jac and Brigit and how you all supported one another in times of crisis. Your loyalty is obvious for all to see."

He swung his hands wide for emphasis. "The pain that you feel at the loss of these two women is reflected in your eyes. But they are not lost. Because you have told me they will seek you out. I will ensure that Ares finds them."

"What?" Rachel's mouth dropped open. Her eyes widened in shock, then outrage. She placed her hands on the table and rose, pushing the chair away in one movement. "Leave Jac and Brigit out of this."

"I cannot do that, my Queen, for their company has been requested."

"By who? I never said—"

"In your mind, you've asked for them dozens of times. I'll stop Ares's quest for the red-devil and send him to wait for your friends instead."

"Ares is the dark-haired man I saw the first day I was brought here, right?" Somehow she just knew that's who he was talking about.

"Yes, he is like a brother."

147

Rachel shivered. Ares gave her the willies. His jade eyes had pierced through her, like a blade, unsettling in their regard. She pictured the dark hunter, then imagined Jac. "No, you can't send him after my friends!" Rachel plopped down on the chair, holding her head. This wasn't happening. Eros had her dead to rights. She may not have said anything aloud, but she thought of Jac and Brigit often. It still wasn't right to inflict this situation upon her friends, *was it*?

She looked up in a flash. "Stay out of my mind," she warned.

"Why do you fight me, when you know what I say is true?"

Rachel covered her face with her hands in frustration. "I'm not fighting you. I just don't...I just don't know what I want anymore." She dropped her hands and looked into his fathomless depths. "You are purposely trying to confuse me."

Eros shrugged. "Tell me about Donald."

The mere mention of the man had Rachel ready to spit bullets. That bastard should pay. But if she stayed here, there was no way justice would be done.

"Justice will be done, my Queen. I will see to it." Eros pushed the table out of the way and pulled Rachel onto his lap. He stroked the side of her hair with his fingers, gently tugging on the loose strands.

She sniffed. "What does that mean?"

"I cannot allow this man to escape the jungle. He is far too much of a threat to my people. Besides he has broken Atlantean law."

"What law?"

"Atlantean law states that if a man strikes a woman in our society he must face a tribunal. If he is found guilty, the group will strip him of his ability to mate, along with his telepathic powers. Once he has lost these powers, he often chooses to leave the tribe and go off to die."

Rachel's jaw dropped. "They'll chop off his dick?"

Eros nodded. "Our methods are humane."

"Then it's not for Donald," she snapped. "He doesn't deserve humane."

"But necessary. We have so few among us, as you may have noticed, that our women are protected above all else. We show them honor and respect, as all societies of the world should."

"Unfortunately the world doesn't work that way."

"I am aware of your world." Eros's jaw tightened.

Rachel shook her head. "The tribunal wouldn't be able to hold a trial for Donald. He's not a telepath and he doesn't mate. Besides, I'd need proof."

"You have it right here in front of you." Eros patted his chest.

Rachel worried her teeth over her lower lip. "You?"

"I witnessed him striking you. No one would doubt the word of the King."

"He's probably halfway back to New York by now."

Eros shrugged. "He will be found," he said without apology or further explanation. "Now let's see the village."

Chapter Twelve

Eros rose, lifting Rachel in the process. He gently set her feet on the floor and led her out the door. His eyes caressed her lovingly, warming her. Rachel figured she would never grow tired of basking in those lipid pools.

He placed her hand on the crook of his arm and put his large palm over top. Rachel felt special. Needed. Wanted. And it scared her senseless.

They walked along the tree branch. The huts were empty. Rachel glanced and saw people bustling on the ground. She tightened her grip on Eros. He patted her hand in reassurance.

Warm, orchid perfumed air clung to her skin, moistening it to a glistening sheen. Rachel looked up, catching glimpses of sunlight through the swaying leaves. A breeze washed over her in a gentle embrace.

Rachel stopped dead, pulling Eros to a halt beside her.

"What is it, my Queen?"

"I..I..I'm naked."

"You are properly clothed."

"I can't go down there like this. People will see my…" Rachel indicated her pierced nipples. "And my…" She pointed down.

Eros laughed. The sound rumbled through her, vibrating the golden hoops. She bit her lip against the sensation.

"It will be fine, my Queen."

She squeezed his arm. "You don't understand. I can't go down there without my clothes."

"Your old clothing is disrespectful in the eyes of the Atlantean people." He turned to face her, his expression serious, as he reached out to gently clutch her arms. "Their feelings would be hurt. You don't want that, do you?"

Rachel shook her head. This was a no-win situation. She didn't want to hurt anyone, certainly not these people who had been so accepting of her presence. But she didn't want to appear almost naked in public. She took a couple of deep breaths, letting them out slowly. Rachel thought of Jac, then squared her shoulders and raised her chin.

Eros smiled and guided her to the transport basket. "I really must meet this woman you call Jac."

He lowered the transport with care, whispering sweet words in praise of Rachel's beauty all the way to the ground. She closed her eyes, allowing herself to bask in the husky timber of his voice, until they safely reached the earthen floor.

"Thank you for the kind words," she said a second before a blush stole over her cheeks.

Eros had trouble tearing his eyes from Rachel's loveliness. "I speak only the truth, my Queen."

She touched his arm tentatively and wrapped her small fingers around his wrist. He placed his hand on top of hers once more. Everything about her felt right. She held her chin high, despite her embarrassment over the prospect of walking through his village naked.

Eros shook his head. The people of this planet had strange ideas about what constituted decency. They were more concerned about proper attire than feeding their people. That was just one of the many reasons he had to get the Atlanteans off planet Earth.

Eros assisted Rachel from the transport. They walked along the perimeter of the camp. He introduced her to the women who were preparing tomorrow night's feast. They were all bare-breasted. Two of the women had been pierced through the nipples, while the third, Cassandra had none. Rachel made a mental note to ask Eros what significance the hoops held in the tribe.

All wore the same kind of long skirt that Rachel had on, but the colors were all different. Three sets of aqua eyes stared at her tentatively. Rachel smiled and shook hands with all the ladies, instantly liking them all, but feeling an immediate bond with Cassandra. Her discomfort fell away as the women of Atlantis embraced her with warmth, sisterly love, and compassion.

After a few moments Eros took her arm once more, and the women turned back to their work. Eros guided Rachel toward the seer's home. They were crossing the final trail when Ares stepped from the jungle blocking the path. Rachel jumped, pressing her body against Eros's wide back in an attempt to hide. *Speak of the devil.*

"All is well, my Queen." Eros grinned at the warrior before him as he spoke to Rachel. "This is my friend, Ares."

Rachel peeked out from behind Eros's waist. She knew who he was. The dark hunter was more intimidating up close than the bogeyman would be. Rachel stared into those piercing eyes, quivering under their intensity. She could feel the heat in her face all the way to her toes. Ares's dark male beauty was breathtaking, but the air of danger surrounding him managed to frighten her anyway.

Hair as black as the grim reaper's cape hung down his back, so straight that it looked as if someone had ironed it. His body, corded with muscle, appeared well worn, with a few scattered scars. It struck Rachel that he was the only Atlantean she'd seen with scars, but the fact seemed oddly fitting. His jade colored eyes sparkled like the finest emeralds. A blade of a nose ran sharply down his striking face. Rachel could feel the leashed power within his large frame, coiled tight and ready to spring free at any moment.

"Come out from behind me so that Ares can give you a proper greeting."

Rachel made a tentative move to her right. She was out from behind Eros, but still a step or two back. She held out her hand. Ares just stared at it for a few seconds, then raised his eyes to Eros.

'Tis her people's custom to shake hands when they meet, Eros said telepathically.

But that is not a proper greeting. What would you have me do?

Eros shrugged. *Shake her hand, then give her a proper Atlantean greeting. But before you do, did the seer speak with you?*

Ares nodded, then shifted uncomfortably.

Eros smiled, but mentioned nothing about his friend's obvious change in demeanor. *What have you learned of the Professor?*

I have found some of his tracks, along with many dead bodies on the trail. At first all appeared to be accidental, but after careful examination I realized they'd all been murdered. He is concealing his deeds. The group has divided. The Professor appears to have headed back to the original campsite but he's covering his tracks well. His trail has all but disappeared. If you wish, I could try to pick it up again and follow him.

Eros shook his head. *I've sent new orders to the seer. I take it you've spoken with Ariel and you'll leave directly after the mating ceremony?*

For a second Ares's muscles tensed and something flashed in his eyes. He looked as if he were about to argue or protest, but then with a kind of feigned resignation he relaxed and nodded instead.

The Queen misses her friends, Eros added. *In her mind she's convinced they will come.*

I will do as I'm commanded, as always.

One last thing, my friend, beware of the one known as Jac. From the Queen's memories, I'd wish the blonde demon on no man.

Ares's jade orbs glinted, but he said nothing.

Rachel knew they were having a conversation. Men just didn't stare at each other in silence, unless they were getting ready to fight. And there didn't seem to be any reason for that to happen. She wanted to ask what they were discussing but decided against it. If they'd been in New York she'd have guessed sports, but what in the hell kind of Atlantean sport could they be discussing…vine climbing? Rachel snorted.

She was about to drop her hand when with lightning speed Ares grasped her palm, dwarfing it in his own. He shook it a couple of times then let go. Rachel was grateful that he'd been quick. The man overwhelmed her. *Whoever he is mated to must be a really strong woman.*

Rachel tried to hide her uneasiness by keeping her hands glued to her sides. She felt extremely exposed in her Atlantean clothing. It didn't help that Ares's eyes kept perusing her, settling more than once upon her nipples. She blushed deeper.

She was about to turn away when Ares dropped to his knees before her. Rachel looked to Eros for guidance. Her head whipped around and she gasped as Ares clasped his hands on her hips.

Rachel shot Eros a pointed stare. "What is he doing?"

Her mouth dropped open as Ares leaned forward. The second his lips made contact, Rachel's body responded of its own volition. Her nipples beaded and tightened under Ares's firm lips.

Rachel's skin heated as his strong, callused fingers held her firm. Her body quivered as he placed another kiss on the opposite nipple, giving a quick flick of his tongue to her gold ring before pulling back. Rachel's channel flooded. Ares inhaled. The smile he shot her was devastating. He *knew* exactly how he'd affected her.

Damn my traitorous body.

Rachel had the urge to wipe that smug grin right off Ares's darkly handsome face. Before she could tell him exactly what she thought of him and his outlandish behavior, Ares spoke, answering the question she'd forgotten she'd asked.

"I am paying proper respect to my new Queen."

Rachel planted her hands on her hips and glared at Eros. "Are you going to let him get away with that?"

"But of course. He pays you proper respect." He shrugged. "If he did not, then there would be a problem."

She didn't miss the wink Eros sent Ares. "But he kissed me on—on—my breasts."

"That is the Atlantean way of proper greeting and a show of respect."

"The women didn't kiss me there."

Eros grinned in an all-too-male-pleased-with-himself sort of way. "'Tis how the men of our species show respect to the women."

Rachel tried to sound calm when she asked the question, but her voice came out wispy and pinched. "Do you kiss the women like that?"

"The new Queen is jealous. A good sign, my King." Ares rose with a full-blown grin across his face.

She stomped her foot. "I am *not* jealous."

"I have upset you, my Queen. For that I am truly sorry. It has been a pleasure to meet you. I look forward to seeing more of you," his eyes wandered over her body in appreciation, "at the feast tomorrow night."

Ares turned away and strode off into the jungle before Rachel could say another word.

"What did he mean by that?"

Eros's innocent expression didn't fool her one bit. "What?"

"When he said he looked forward to seeing *more* of me tomorrow night?"

"Ares will be part of the ceremony. 'Tis nothing." Eros shrugged, but she noticed he avoided eye contact while answering her.

Suspicion sank into her gut, taking up permanent residence. Rachel didn't believe Ares's involvement in the ceremony was nothing. It certainly didn't feel like nothing. She crossed her arms over her chest. She'd let it go for now, but she wasn't about to forget it. She enjoyed being out of the hut and in the fresh, albeit muggy air.

Rachel would have never thought that walking around topless in a see-through skirt would be erotic, but it was. The brush of the material against her bare pussy, the slight movement the rings in her nipples made when she inhaled, all wreaked havoc on her sensitive skin. There was a certain freedom that came with nudity, and despite her misgivings she found the whole thing titillating. She'd had to stop a couple of times for fear she'd orgasm right on the trail.

Her eyes strayed to Eros's lean form. His legs flexed as he walked, splitting into corded muscles. His loincloth separated with each long stride, exposing glimpses of his tight, rounded ass. She watched his biceps curl and flex as he pointed out different buildings and their functions in the encampment.

A thin sheen of sweat coated his body, giving him a golden glow. His musky scent surrounded her, enticing, luring and subtly inviting her to touch his hard form. Rachel's mouth went dry and she coughed. All of her thoughts turned carnal in Eros's presence.

"Tell me about Atlantis," she asked, trying to ignore her body's animal urges.

"In the beginning, Atlantis was no different than other warring nations. As technology grew, so did the peace movement among the people." Eros paused at the edge of the jungle to pick an orchid growing on one of the trees. He handed the bloom to Rachel. "We realized that with new developments came greater dangers, so the sages took precautions to prevent disaster. But it was too late…"

"Why?" Rachel spun the stem of the bloom in her hand, before inhaling the sweet intoxicating fragrance.

"The damage had been done to the environment."

"What happened?"

"My people weren't from Earth, but from Zaron. We colonized Atlantis many millennia ago. When a few of the wiser sages realized Atlantis was in danger, they met to devise a transport system to return us to our home planet."

Eros took a deep breath, as if gathering strength to continue. "They developed an advanced technology out of fire-crystals. These held such awesome power that several of the sages feared they could not be controlled." Eros watched a pair of monkeys playing in the trees. The tension stretched his body into a tight cord, making each breath labored. Rachel waited, giving him the time needed to continue.

Finally he turned to face her, his gaze softening. "The transport succeeded and many of our people made it off the planet. But before the sages could transport the remaining Atlanteans, a volcano erupted, causing a tidal wave to bury our continent beneath the sea."

"I'm sorry, Eros." Rachel put her hand on his shoulder in reassurance.

"So many deaths." Eros's gaze clouded. He still stood in front of her, but in his mind he was a million miles away reliving the horror. "So much screaming." His body flinched and his sensuous mouth twisted into a bitter slash. "My parents sent me, along with all the other children they could find, through the portal with the four remaining fire-crystals and the stone symbols. But with the collapse came a malfunction in the machine. We ended up here in this jungle."

She squeezed his hand in silent support. "Can I see the ruins?"

Eros led Rachel from the village. They walked for about ten minutes in comfortable silence. Rachel caught glimpses of parrots in the trees. Monkeys chattered as they swung from branch to branch, their playful cries sounding like noisy, excited children at recess.

The jungle smelled green and alive. Rachel never knew the earth had such a strong distinctive odor. She hadn't slowed down long enough in New York to notice. Every once in a while the air shifted and she caught the scent of Eros, his skin a tempting aphrodisiac to her senses.

The path narrowed, becoming dense with overgrown vegetation. Leaves brushed Rachel's bare skin, sending delicious shivers down her spine. Sunlight dappled her face and arms. The weight of the gold hoops was just enough to tease the nerve endings in her nipples, causing them to pebble and ache.

Rachel lifted the edge of the skirt to step over vines. The material brushed over her thighs and gooseflesh rose on her legs. Her eyes darted to Eros's big hands, then across his smooth, glistening, broad back. It didn't take long for her imagination to kick into high gear.

She could almost feel those rough palms covering her breasts, molding, as he brought her eager nipples to his hungry mouth. The moisture between her legs grew as she pictured Eros's thick cock, throbbing as he positioned the plum size crown at her entrance. Her clit pulsed and she bit back a moan.

Rachel glanced up in time to see Eros's step falter. His breathing had deepened and his gait was awkward as he continued down the trail. His skin held a slight flush. When he stepped over a felled branch, Rachel caught sight of the massive hard-on under his loincloth. She licked her lips, then blushed, realizing he'd been listening to her private musings. At first the thought angered her, but the anger soon faded, quickly replaced by sexual energy.

For the first time in her life she felt powerful, feminine, all woman. Rachel couldn't prevent the grin that stole across her face. It was a heady feeling knowing her thoughts, emotions, and form held sway over Eros's larger than life body.

Hidden deep within the jungle they came upon a man-made clearing. The energy in the air crackled like when a storm neared. The hair on her arms stood on end and the hoops at her nipples vibrated. Rachel's body trembled as if an internal power struggle had begun. Her head spun and her stomach churned for a few minutes while she fought to control her equilibrium.

This ground held the power of life and death, good and evil, yin and yang. Black lava rocks were strewn about the area and four large red crystals lay on their sides toppled by an unseen force.

Eros walked to her side and placed his arm around her shoulder, enveloping her in his strength. His loving touch settled her. "These are the symbols I told you about." He pointed to the lava rocks.

Rachel walked up to one. At first glance they appeared to be ordinary volcanic rocks, but upon further examination she discovered symbols etched on the sides. She picked up the first rock, turning it slowly so as not to miss any part of the glyph. Her brows furrowed as she returned the piece to its original resting spot. Rachel gathered two more stones, placing them by the first. She rotated each symbol back and forth until they fit together like a jigsaw puzzle.

"I think I might be able to read this once I get it pieced together." Rachel glanced over her shoulder at Eros.

He nodded his head and smiled. "Good."

Rachel and Eros retrieved all the pieces scattered about the ground and brought them back to the original three.

"It's going to take me a while to figure out what piece goes where," Rachel said vaguely as she considered the rocks. "Even then, who knows if I'll be able to understand what the symbols mean."

Eros picked up one of the rocks and ran his fingers along the design. "How long do you need?"

She shrugged. "A month, maybe longer. It depends."

Eros continued to examine the stone in his hand.

Rachel walked over to one of the fire crystals several yards away. The minerals reflecting in the sunlight gave off a flawless prism. She was about to return to Eros's side when she noticed a yellow flower growing at the base.

She picked a few buds and held them up to her face. The flowers smelled spicy like cinnamon, but with a strange lingering odor, as if they held an aftertaste. Rachel couldn't seem to get enough of the addictive scent.

"What are these?" She held the blooms up for Eros to see.

She watched his color drain. "Where did you get them?" His voice cracked with emotion.

Rachel felt her skin flush and her pussy begin to ache. "At the base of the crystal."

His eyes bulleted to her hand, then face. "Did you smell those?"

"Yeah, why?" Her nipples beaded and throbbed. "What's happening to me?" she cried out, dropping the blooms to the ground.

Eros rushed to her side. "You have inhaled the Atlantean bama plant."

"What does that mean?" she asked as the plant began to affect her nervous system. She reached out and grabbed Eros. "Please, help me," she gasped, tugging her skirt off with a jerky motion, unable to stand the material next to her heated skin.

Rachel couldn't seem to control her actions. It was as if she'd been possessed. She began to rub her body against Eros's hard length. She was wet, needy, out of control with desire. Her fingers snaked down his chest, along his flat stomach, slipping beneath his loincloth, until she grasped his cock.

Eros jumped, but didn't pull away. "The bama plant only grows here, near the crystals. It aids in building desire. My people brought the seeds with them from Atlantis. The blooms were never meant to be inhaled by an ordinary human." Every muscle in his body clenched.

"Are you saying the plant makes you horny?" she rasped out.

Rachel's fingers clasped the base of Eros's cock, working their way up and down, stroking, gliding, taunting. He nodded, his breathing coming out in rapid pants.

"How long does it last?" She trailed kisses over his chest, a second before she slipped one of his nipples, ring and all, in her mouth. Rachel suckled at him, sliding her tongue back and forth over the hoop, probing the flat disc.

Eros groaned. "It depends," he bit out, "on how much you inhaled." She swirled and licked. Eros's knees buckled and he dropped to the grass, taking Rachel with him.

She ground her hips against him, leaving a trail of moisture behind. "Make it stop."

He shuddered. "I can't without joining with you."

"Then fuck me, for goodness sake," she pleaded, incapable of understanding why that was such a bad idea.

"I can't," he rasped. "The ceremony…my people."

What was he talking about? Rachel attempted to grasp onto his reason for about two seconds before her body's clawing need ripped all thought from her head. From that moment on, all she knew was that she couldn't seem to get close enough to him and he resisted.

Her fevered body demanded release. Rachel pushed Eros onto his back with her free hand and straddled him. She let go of his cock long enough to strip him of the loincloth. Then she grasped him again, trying to guide his cock to her drenched channel. Her clit twitched, causing her to cry out.

"Please, Eros…"

She rubbed her pussy along his hard length, grinding her body against him. Eros reached out, lifting her from him far enough away to roll her under his heavy bulk. She released his cock.

He thrust hard against her, grinding his shaft into the sensitive nub between her legs. Sweat beaded his brow as his tongue sought out her nipples. He nipped and sucked, his movements urgent, primal—frantic. Her areolas stabbed out, engorged. His cock slipped into place, ready to ram into her moist entrance.

Eros froze. The breath left his body. He balanced on fate's precipice—once crossed, it could not be undone. Rachel tried to scoot down and impale herself on his shaft. Eros held her firm, his entire body shaking with the effort. His people depended on his self-control. He wanted to fuck her more than he wanted his next breath.

"Rachel please," he begged. "You know not what you ask."

She bucked her hips into his and the head of his cock slid inside her. Her vaginal walls gripped him, pulled at him, urging him forward. She felt like heaven on earth, slick and hot, moist and welcoming, and oh so tight. Eros groaned and closed his eyes, begging the goddess for strength. His massive body shook, while every fiber in his being screamed to thrust—to claim.

The demon voice in his head taunted him to seek his release, while giving Rachel hers.

But he couldn't. He had to be strong.

Eros pulled back and rolled away from Rachel. His great lungs labored for breath. A pearl of liquid seeped from his crown, mingling with her essence, glistening in the sunlight.

Rachel swooped down upon him like a scavenger, her lips forming a tight seal around his cock. Instantly Eros shuddered, spurting seed deep within her throat. The flow so great he thought it might never stop. He'd been that close to ruining any chance his people had to escape the planet. After she'd swallowed every drop, she sat up, her eyes glazed, incoherent.

Eros spread Rachel onto the grass. Her legs fell open, exposing her wet pussy to his hungry gaze. He swooped down, covering her mound with his ravishing mouth. He licked and suckled at her clit until she was mindless. She orgasmed, but still her body ached. She wanted more, needed more, demanded all.

He plunged his tongue inside her dripping channel, stretching its length until he reached her womb, then he curled the lengthy muscle back, repeating the action over and over again. Finally he thrust forward and hummed, sending an energy surge from his tongue into her velvet grip.

Rachel screamed, her body shattering its second release. Eros twisted his tongue in a quick corkscrew fashion and she came again. He swirled around her inner walls, until Rachel grew hoarse from crying out. Her limbs trembled and shook as the effects of one orgasm after the other rolled through her, blending into endless sensation. He laved her clit mercilessly.

Her breathing was ragged, but her body felt sated for the first time since inhaling the pollen of the bama plant. They lay side-by-side, watching butterflies dance in the air. Rachel propped herself up on her elbow and looked down into Eros's strained face.

Rachel felt ashamed by her behavior. Never in all her years of dating had she ever acted the sexual aggressor. It was easier to believe it had only been the bama plant affecting her and not some baser desire she'd kept hidden away. "I'm sorry. I—"

He held up a hand, stopping her words. "'Tis my fault. Had I not been lost in the past, this never would have happened."

"But you said something about your people..."

"All is well. We stopped before we could join fully." Eros sat up and pulled Rachel to her feet. He helped her slip her skirt back on.

"I don't understand."

"You will."

She ran a shaky hand through her tangled hair, before taking one last look around the clearing. In the future, Rachel would stay far away from the harmless looking yellow flowers.

Eros nodded, a solemn look upon his handsome features. "'Tis time you meet the seer." He brushed his palms on his loincloth, before grabbing Rachel's hand and leading her away.

Rachel was torn. One side wanted to go home to New York and her friends more than anything in the world. The other was so fascinated with the lava rocks and the secrets that they held that she couldn't wait to get started in trying to decode them. For the time being, she'd leave the fire-crystals untouched. But that would mean staying here, for at least a month, possibly much longer.

Rachel pulled her hand free. "Eros, how old did you say those symbols on the lava rocks are?"

"Over two and a half thousand years, give or take. When the sages created them, the stones they used were already four thousand years old, according to legend."

She blinked at him. "That would make you two thousand years old."

"A bit over a two, but who's counting." He laughed.

Rachel stared at him. Her mind tried to wrap around the information he'd just so casually shared with her. She didn't like being made a fool of, especially by a man she was beginning to care for. Not many people reached a hundred years old, much less two thousand.

He grabbed her hand once more. "Come, my Queen, 'tis time for you to meet the seer."

In all likelihood the man holding her hand was insane. *But what if he was telling the truth*? She should be frightened, but she wasn't. Rachel glanced at their intertwined fingers, then to Eros's profile. Physically he was her ideal, but mentally was a whole different ballgame.

Sweat from his body caused a musky scent to linger in the air, mingling with hers. Rachel inhaled, taking in the pleasing odor.

Warmth emanated from his fingers, spreading throughout her body. Rachel found the contact strangely comforting. He really was a magnificent looking man. The fact that it felt so right to be with him…well, perhaps the prospect of staying here wasn't so scary after all.

Chapter Thirteen

Eros led her to the seer's hut. His emotions had jumbled once he felt the shift in acceptance radiating from Rachel. He should have been ecstatic, but instead he shuddered at the thought of how close he'd come to betraying his people back in the clearing. When the tip of his cock had sought and found Rachel's slick entrance, it had given Eros a taste of heaven on Earth. How could the goddess cruelly tempt him so?

He'd wanted Rachel so bad that he'd almost willingly thrown away his future and the future of his people just to be able to bury himself between her silken thighs. After the bama plant ordeal, when she'd looked up at him from the jungle floor where they lay, her eyes had shown clearly the love that simmered in her heart. Eros felt as if he would burst with joy.

They snaked their way along the trail until they reached the entrance to the seer's hut. Eros held up his hand and his palm glowed. He prayed the seer had words of wisdom to share. He needed all the strength he could get.

Rachel remembered the first time she'd seen that occur. At the time, she'd chalked it up to imagination, but now there was no mistaking the power emanating from Eros.

Perhaps he had told the truth — *about everything.*

It only took a moment for Ariel the seer to throw back her furs to grant them entrance. She opened her arms wide, enveloping Rachel in a welcoming hug. "Finally we meet, my Queen." She pulled back, but still kept a hold on Rachel's upper arm. Her gaze ran from the top of Rachel's head all the way to her toes. "You are even lovelier than my visions."

Rachel blushed. "Thank you."

"Eros." The seer turned to him. "Please wait outside. I need to discuss a few things about the ceremony with our new Queen."

"As you wish, Ariel." Eros hesitated.

Rachel gave him a reassuring smile.

"I'll summon you when 'tis time for you to return," Ariel added.

He nodded and left.

Rachel watched as the woman known as the seer released her arm and walked to the other side of her hut. The woman was beautiful beyond words. Her long blonde hair hung in soft waves down her back. She had full breasts and a slim waist. She seemed at ease, comfortable in her nudity.

Her features were delicate. Her upturned nose looked pert set against her high cheekbones. Her well-shaped brows framed her aqua eyes, reminding Rachel of two perfect reefs surrounded by tropical waters. The bow of her mouth would make even the most skilled plastic surgeon envious.

Rachel squelched the need to cover herself. Why hadn't Eros chosen Ariel for his mate? She seemed perfect in every way.

Ariel chuckled, momentarily covering her mouth with her hand. She glanced back at Rachel. "Your name is Dr. Rachel Evans, yet you are not a doctor of medicine."

Rachel rubbed her hands along her arms, trying to brush away her insecurities. "I received my degrees in anthropology and linguistics. I specialize in ancient civilizations and extinct languages."

Ariel smiled. "Then you are perfect."

Rachel tried not to laugh. "Perfect?" The woman before her obviously hadn't looked in a mirror lately.

"For the King. For all of us." Ariel walked to the corner of her hut and opened a tiny cabinet. She pulled out a flask and emptied the contents into a couple of cups that looked to be carved from huingo fruit. The liquid, thick and yellow, reminded Rachel of banana yogurt. Ariel handed Rachel a cup and then raised hers up in a mock salute.

Rachel sniffed a couple of times, but couldn't place the sweet odor. "What is this?"

"'Tis a fruit that grows only within the boundaries of the village. Drink, 'tis quite delicious." Ariel's eyes were locked on Rachel's face, waiting.

Feeling like a mouse trapped in a cat's clutches, Rachel brought the cup to her lips, but hesitated. The seer took a big gulp and then smiled once again. Rachel watched as the column of Ariel's throat worked to swallow the thick drink, then she raised her cup to her lips and took a sip. The juice tasted sweet, yet tangy with a nutty aftertaste. She took another drink.

Without warning, she felt lightheaded. The sparsely furnished room began to spin.

"What...what was in that?" Rachel tried to reach out and grab the seer but she seemed to swim in and out of her vision.

"Ayahausca. 'Tis a simple plant drug that will allow you to foretell the future. Perhaps see your true feelings. Like the way you were able to see Eros in your dreams."

"You drugged me?"

Ariel reached down and removed the cup from Rachel's grasp. "I apologize, my Queen, but tomorrow night's ceremony is too important. You must be ready to accept your rightful place."

According to Rachel's drugged out eyes, there were now three Ariels floating about the hut. "You bitch. I'm gonna...I'm gonna..." Rachel slumped forward and saw the table closing in about a second before her head made contact.

Then all went black.

* * * * *

A kaleidoscope of colors swirled around Rachel's head, followed by lightning like streaks of light. Her stomach spun as if she were on a tilt-a-whirl ride. The colors whirled and melded before her eyes until they formed solid objects.

Eros stood in a field of blue flowers. The sky was green. Orange moons dotted the horizon. Strange looking creatures resembling oversized butterflies cruised overhead. Their flapping wings created a gentle breeze and perfumed the already fragrant air.

We're not in Kansas anymore. Her mind fought to keep up with what she was seeing.

Eros squatted down, his arms held out in front of him. Rachel looked over her shoulder. Two children, a golden-haired boy and a brunette girl, raced past Rachel, smiling and giggling. Eros scooped the kids up and spun around in circles, hugging them close. Their excited squeals sent the butterfly creatures scattering.

Rachel smiled. Eros looked so happy. Her heart tugged as she saw the love written on his face, shining in his eyes. These were his children. She averted her eyes, tears forming on her lashes. The beauty of the moment overwhelmed her. Eros made such a wonderful father.

She looked around, but there seemed to be no mother. A lump formed in her throat. *Those should be our kids.* She turned back to the idyllic scene. The family of three stared in her direction.

Rachel glanced over her shoulder—a ship sat on a runway, waiting to blast off and take her home. She turned back. Eros and the children spread their arms wide and smiled. The innocent gesture spoke volumes.

The decision was hers to make.

Rachel took one last look at the ship. Everything she knew—her job and her friends—waited for her in New York.

But if she left here, she'd lose all that really mattered.

The realization slammed her in the gut.

She wanted to be part of the picture he presented. She wanted those kids. She wanted Eros.

* * * * *

Rachel awoke with a start. Her head throbbed and she felt as if someone had run her through a spin cycle. Eros had his hand resting on her shoulder. His face was pinched with worry. Something inside Rachel melted. She tried to give him a smile, but grimaced instead.

Eros brushed the hair away from her face, his fingers featherlike on her skin. "Are you well?" His voice, low and deep, broke with unchecked emotions.

Rachel looked around, her eyes finding Ariel. She shot the seer a lethal look. "You don't play fair."

"I do what is best for my King and my people," Ariel said casually before adding, "and you."

Eros and Rachel left the seer's hut to find the sun had disappeared from the sky. Stars twinkled. A fire blazed in the center of the compound, crackling with new life each time a fresh log caught on. Night creatures stirred in the brush and the air hung cloak-like, blanketing all. Trees whispered promises of a cool breeze. Insects buzzed and croaked, swallowing the stillness of the night.

"How long was I out?" she muttered more to herself than to him.

Eros had refused to let her walk on her own. His strong fingers clasped her hand. The rough pad of his thumb brushed the back of her knuckles sending warmth through Rachel's groggy body. She leaned into his broad shoulders for support.

Glancing her way, his eyes roamed over her face. Concern etched his forehead. "You were in vision for hours."

She shook her head. It had seemed like only a couple of minutes had passed. The scene in the field refused to leave Rachel's mind. They had been so happy as a family.

Damn that Ariel.

More images from the dream flooded in. There had been several moons in the sky, or perhaps planets. Rachel hadn't paid that much attention to them.

Maybe Ariel gave me a hallucinogenic and planted the vision in my mind?

But she didn't think so. The more she considered the scene, the more Rachel was convinced she hadn't been on Earth.

"What time is it?"

"The hour is late," he said, raising his head to the sky.

"Did you know Ariel planned to drug me?"

Eros's step faltered. "I did not know the seer was going to use the Spirit Vine on you. Ariel's methods are not discussed amongst our people. I trust her to do what's best."

Rachel paused. Her eyes searched Eros's face to confirm his sincerity. She blew out a ragged breath and ran a hand over her face, trying to clear her head. "I had a dream."

"Do you wish to share the dream?" His calm tone seemed to belie his true emotions.

Rachel knew the question was not casual. He was asking her for so much more. She stopped when they reached the center of the compound. "I figured you'd already taken a look inside my head to see," she snapped.

He flinched. "No. I would never intrude on a vision. Contrary to what you believe, I'm not in the habit of intruding on private thoughts."

"But?"

Eros held up a hand to halt her speech. "The circumstances are different with you, my Rachel. You are to be my Queen. You are human. I am not. I must get to know you better than perhaps you know yourself."

Rachel stared at him. Every time she thought she had him figured out, he'd surprise her. "I don't think I was on Earth in the dream."

Eros heaved in a surprised breath. "What did you see?"

"Planets or moons, I'm not sure. There were several in the sky. And strange butterfly-like creatures." She didn't tell him about the children. She wasn't ready to share that information with anyone until she decided how she felt.

Eros shook his head. "I believe you were on Zaron, the planet where the people of Atlantis originated. What else did you see?"

"Nothing," she bit out.

Eros didn't press her for more information, which was just as well. She felt raw, edgy, exposed by the dream.

"We should take nourishment." Eros tugged her to a table set up at the side of the fire. It was filled with various foods.

Rachel's lips pursed as she rubbed her stomach. "It's funny. I really haven't been hungry since I arrived here in the village."

"That is common. The energy fields are strong around the compound due to the fire-crystals. Your body gains most of its nourishment through the air. 'Tis still important to eat occasionally to keep your organs functioning properly."

"Wow, that's so cool." Rachel's eyes widened as she thought of the possibilities. "It's like the perfect diet. You'd make a fortune selling it to the outside world."

Eros's expression turned cold. "The people of this planet would destroy themselves, just as we did in Atlantis."

Rachel pictured the devastation, the greed and wars that would occur as countries tried to get their hands on the technology. "You're right. This can never leave your village. It would spell the end of the world as we know it."

Dr. Donald flashed in her mind. For once, Rachel was glad he was long gone.

* * * * *

Creeping through the jungle with a couple of guides, the Professor came upon tracks. The feet were large, leaving no room for error in classifying the species. They had been followed, like he'd suspected. He bristled when he thought about Dr. Rachel Evans and how he'd let her escape. The bitch had made a great discovery. She'd uncovered a lost tribe.

Whoever these people turned out to be, they were as adept in the trees as well as on ground. Their village would be the discovery of a lifetime and he would get all the credit. He'd send a man on ahead to scout the area while he returned to the drop site to wait for a plane to take him back to New York. He'd need more resources before proceeding.

Donald snickered as the tracker Jaro disappeared into the jungle. The guide could find the village and Dr. Evans, killing two birds with one stone.

Chapter Fourteen

Eros and Rachel ate their dinner in silence. The breadfruit had been carefully prepared with roasted fish and mangos. Any other time Rachel would have considered the meal delicious, but tonight she just couldn't concentrate on the food. All that ran through her mind was the dream and the mating ceremony.

Eros stared down at the food in his bowl. "I must leave tonight." He picked up a piece of fruit and brought it to Rachel's lips.

She frowned and took his offering into her mouth. Rachel sucked the juices from Eros's fingertips. She saw his face flush with color and he shifted in his seat. She didn't want Eros to go.

Perhaps if I torment him enough, he'll stay.

Rachel tore off a piece of bread and held it in front of her, inviting, tempting, daring him to bite. Her fingers trembled as Eros closed his hand around hers, pulling her from her seat and onto his lap.

His tongue snaked out as he licked the length of her fingers. She felt an answering wetness pool at the juncture of her thighs. Her nipples peaked against the warmth of his chest. He bit off a piece of the bread and then smiled, an unholy light sparking fire in his eyes.

Rachel snuggled in close, wanting the connection. "Why must you leave?"

"'Tis customary for the soon-to-be-mated couple to spend the night before the ceremony apart."

"Just like when a person is married where I come from. Not that I'd know." Rachel gave Eros a nervous smile. "I've never been married before."

"I, also, have never been through the mating ceremony." He reached out and grabbed her hand, giving it a quick squeeze. "We aren't allowed to mate, unless the seer confirms a union in her vision."

"You mean you've never had sex?" Rachel couldn't hide the shock and disbelief running through her voice. Her gaze roamed over his body. "I don't believe it."

Eros laughed. "Of course I've had sex."

"What's so funny?" Unwilling to meet his gaze, her face flushed. She leapt from Eros's lap. Her hands flew to her hips and she began tapping her toe in aggravation.

Eros reached out and pulled her back on his lap.

She refused to look at him.

He turned her chin, until she faced him. "There is a big difference between having sex and taking a mate with my people."

"I don't understand."

"Sexual pleasure is shared with another unmated Atlantean to fulfill a basic need or to alleviate tension. Once the seer decrees that your mate has arrived, all joining must stop." He dropped his hand onto her leg and began massaging the area. "I have not slid my cock into any woman's cunt since donning the claiming symbols." He reached up and flicked the gold hoops at his nipples.

"So that's what the hoops are for." Rachel shook her head back and forth in confusion. "You're telling me you haven't fucked anyone since we met."

"I have not joined with another. That is correct." Eros paused as if trying to search for the right words. "In Atlantean society, you can only have children with your true mate."

"What about unplanned pregnancies?"

He threw his head back. Blond hair cascaded over his muscled chest and down his shoulders. "There are none."

"But that's impossible."

"You don't understand," he said patiently. "The males of my species are not fertile until their mates are found. Our bodies know when 'tis right."

Rachel thought about all the people she'd been introduced to today. She couldn't recall seeing a single child. "You can't have babies."

Eros nodded. "Once a mate has been found, no other will ever do. If anything happens to your mate, then so ends your family's bloodline." His eyes lasered in on Rachel's face and he lowered his voice to almost a whisper. "Atlantean males mate for life."

Rachel couldn't believe her ears. Surely there had to be some kind of loophole for the King. "You mean you can't get married again if I leave, or have children?"

"No, it means I won't." Eros looked into the fire.

"But why?" Her mind raced frantically in search of an answer to this dilemma.

Eros stood up, a lazy smile playing on his sensual mouth. He set her upon her feet. The hand on her leg stilled. He reached out and cupped the side of her face with his palm, stroking the soft outline of her lips with his thumb. "Don't you understand, Rachel? You are all that I want in this lifetime." He paused, his body trembling with emotion. "You are my life, my love, my destiny. Without you, I have no kingdom to rule. I have nothing."

Rachel was stunned. *So that was why he'd fought the urge to fuck her when she'd inhaled the bama plant.* It all made sense now. She'd never been anyone's love, much less destiny. Her heart sang out in joy. Happiness flooded her, threatening to overflow.

"I'll escort you to the hut." Eros walked her from the table and to the transport.

When they reached the hut, he undressed her, letting the skirt slip to the floor, then tucked her naked body into bed. He kissed her forehead, his lips lingering warm against her skin.

"I must go now. Sleep well, my Queen." Eros turned and strode to the door. He glanced over his shoulder at her one last time, then left.

Rachel lay in the bed of furs, unable to move or even think straight. The soft tufts caressed her body, fevering her skin. She squirmed deeper under the covers and drifted off to sleep. She tossed and turned as she dreamed of Eros and their children, of planets beyond the stars, and of Jac and Brigit.

A crash nearby brought her out of her fitful sleep. Rachel sat up, her breath coming in heavy pants. She listened. Silence.

What had awakened her?

She slid off the furs and threw on her skirt. Her eyes tried desperately to make out the shadows in the room.

Suddenly she saw movement. A subtle flash told her someone was in the hut with her. Rachel backed up until her shoulders hit the wall. From the size of the shadow, she could tell it wasn't Eros. He was too small. The man lunged across the room, his hand closing over her mouth before she could get a sound out. His skin smelled of burnt flesh, causing her to gag.

He brought his face next to her ear and she recognized Jaro's voice as he spoke. "If you scream, we'll kill everyone in this entire village. We've set charges and they'll go off if I squeeze this detonator." His words brought a shiver to Rachel's spine as her gaze latched onto something round and metal in his hand. He shoved the object in his pocket before she got a good look. She couldn't chance resisting, too many lives were at stake.

Jaro dragged her to the entrance of the hut. One hand clamped on her mouth, while the other fondled her nipple ring. His touch made her skin crawl. His thick lips brushed against her ear once again. "Maybe you and I will have a little fun later on, since you've caused me so much trouble. I about never got around that dark haired bastard that tracks with more stealth than a panther, but hopefully the false trails I've created will keep him busy long enough to give us some privacy. We didn't get to finish what we started before, remember?"

Rachel's stomach lurched in revulsion. He spoke of Ares. The full moon splashed across his face as he dragged her toward the transport. Anger coursed through her veins. She wouldn't allow this man to lay a finger on her without a fight.

She'd go quietly, for now, if only to protect Eros and his people.

The man lowered them down to the ground in the transport basket. The village was abnormally quiet. The man pulled Rachel along, across the clearing to the edge of the jungle, out of sight of the huts. He dropped his hand from her breast, grabbing her arm instead, as they stepped into the thick shrubs.

He dragged her deeper and deeper into the jungle. "Where are you taking me, you ass?" she pressed out from behind his palm.

"The Professor has paid me well to track you." Jaro yanked hard on her arm, causing her to stumble into him. "He said if I find the village, that I can keep the fair woman for myself."

"Donald is here?"

"No. He will return soon."

"You can't do this."

"But I have, *perra*." Jaro reached up and pinched her nipple ring between his fingers. Hard.

Rachel winced in pain.

He dropped his hand from her breast. "You will get used to how I touch you soon enough."

"No!" Rachel pulled back with all her strength, knocking Jaro off balance. He released her and she fell back onto the ferns. Her elbow struck the ground, sending painful needlelike sensations up her arm.

She scrambled on her hands and knees, trying to gain her feet. Her heart slammed hard against her ribs, pummeling her from the inside. Twigs and plants scraped her skin, tearing the tender flesh. A rock bit into her palm. A jagged cry ripped from her throat. Her long skirt bunched and twisted around her knees, crippling her escape. Jaro pounced on her from behind, pinning her to the ground. His body reeked of dried sweat and stale clothing.

"Maybe I fuck you here." His breath came out in labored puffs. The smell of alcohol permeated the area.

She felt him fumbling with the front of his pants and heard the material of her skirt rip. His zipper scraped her bare bottom as he released his semi-flaccid prick. Rachel's heart pounded so loud she couldn't hear herself think. The man stabbed at her from behind, trying to gain entrance. She attempted to move but couldn't.

Terrified, she tried to scream. A thick hand reached around her and grabbed a handful of dirt and leaves. He shoved them into her mouth, choking off her pleas.

Rachel cried as he found her opening, the sound of her sobs muffled as the man pushed her face into the earth. She closed her eyes, trying to shut out what was to come next, waiting for him to violently plunge inside her.

She thought of Eros and how his touch had been so kind, gentle and loving. Tears stung her eyes. She whimpered against the muddy ground.

The man abruptly stilled, and then his full weight collapsed on her back.

Rachel felt something wet trickle down the side of her face. There was no sound. She spit out the debris. Her lungs burned as she tried to drag in breath. Suddenly the man was removed. Rachel lay on the ground naked and trembling, afraid to look or move a muscle. Her body jerked, racked with sobs. She felt herself being lifted into strong arms.

"Are you okay, my Queen?"

Somewhere in Rachel's mind she recognized Ares's strong voice. He set her upon her feet, his arm resting on her shoulder. Rachel hiccupped and snuggled closer to his warmth. "Is he dead?"

"Yes."

Rachel looked down at the still body lying on a blanket of ferns. She swallowed hard at how close Jaro had come to violating her. The skirt Eros gave her lay nearby in tatters.

Her brows furrowed. "Where is Eros?"

Ares gaze focused on the trail. "He is in the jungle, preparing for the ceremony tomorrow." The muscles in his face were pulled tight in a harsh mask.

Rachel lips formed a silent "O". She wrapped her arms around her waist, hugging herself as tremors racked her body. "Before we leave, check his pockets. He said they'd planted explosives around the campsite."

"The man lied. He was alone in his actions." A tic worked Ares's strong jaw and tiny lines etched deep around his grim mouth. "Did the man," Ares paused, drawing in a ragged breath, his voice harsh against the unnatural silence, "violate you?"

Rachel let out a wail that could wake the dead. Ares held her closer. "Please, my Queen. I must know. If I did not arrive in time, it will be my shame to bear." His body quaked as he waited for her answer.

Rachel sniffled a couple times. Before tonight, she'd feared Ares, but he'd shown his true self and she liked what she saw. He was fierce and brave as a warrior should be. And he'd saved her.

She released his neck. She could feel Ares's heart racing beneath her palms. He was frightened, too.

"You kept him from raping me." Rachel pushed her hair away from her face with trembling fingers. Her eyes sought Ares. "For that I am forever in your debt." She managed a smile.

Ares let go of the breath he'd been holding. Rachel felt his muscles relax as the tension eased. She reached into Jaro's pocket and pulled out a round, silver lighter. *So that's what he'd used to fool her into believing he had a detonator.* Rachel clutched it, pouring all her anger and fear into the object. Ares scooped her up, cradling her near, as he snaked his way through the jungle, backtracking the route the crafty native had taken. He carried Rachel's naked body across the compound to the basket, placing her gently inside.

Once they reached the treetops he picked her up again, taking her to Eros's hut. He pushed aside the fur and walked to the bed. He laid her down, and his trembling hand brushed across her forehead. "Sleep, my Queen. I will stand guard outside."

He turned to leave, but Rachel placed her fingers on his arm, stopping him.

"Thank you. For everything."

He nodded. Ares walked to the fire pot on the table and stuck his hand out. It began to glow. Embers in the pot ignited and burst into flame. "Now you can see everything in the room."

He lifted the fur covering the door. Rachel called out, "Ares, can we keep this between ourselves? I don't want to worry Eros."

"He must know that the outsiders are here," he stated matter of factly, "but 'tis not necessary for him to know the reasons for the guide's death, if that is your wish."

"Thank you." Rachel gave him a half smile and lay back on the furs. Her eyes glanced at the glowing pot. He'd made her a nightlight.

Ares left the hut. As promised he stayed outside, watching for any other sign of trouble. She heard him climb up onto the roof, and his movement as he paced. His footsteps brought her comfort and eventually the solace of sleep.

Chapter Fifteen

The next morning, Rachel woke with her hair matted to her head. She walked to the bucket of water and gasped when she caught a glimpse of her reflection in the liquid. Dried blood crusted in her hair and down the side of her face. Mud and twigs stuck out from her curls and around her ears. Her mouth remained swollen and one of her eyes was black.

She looked like a train wreck.

Rachel scooped up water and tried to scrub away any lingering odor of the man that had attacked her. She felt dirty. Her eyes burned from lack of sleep. She didn't think she could bear to face Eros this morning. Her naked body was bruised, battered. Angry red scratches ran the length of her arms from where she'd fallen.

The flap to the hut opened and Ares stepped through, carrying a new outfit in his hands. "My Queen." He placed the clothing on a chair and walked across the floor to where she stood. He dropped to his knees before her.

Rachel backed away and started to cry, wrapping her arms around herself in an attempt to conceal her nudity. "Please don't." She shook her head, hot tears blurring her eyes and streaming down her cheeks. "I can't go through with the ceremony. Look at me."

Ares raised his eyes, taking in all her cuts and scrapes. "Please allow me to cleanse and heal you."

"You can't take care of all this." She waved her hand in the air before hugging herself once more.

"Please, my Queen." He gently pulled her hands away from her body and kissed each nipple.

His lips were soft and moist against her skin. Rachel's nipples beaded in response to his tender touch. She looked from her breasts to Ares's eyes, the heat rising to her face. "I'm sorry."

"Don't be. 'Tis perfectly natural to respond to a gentle touch."

When he rose, he put his hands on her shoulders. Warmth shot out of them and through her body, heating every inch of her, and she realized he was healing her wounds.

She started to sweat. Ares continued his healing. The palms of his hands glowed bright against her skin, radiating energy. The bruises began to fade until they disappeared, leaving not a mar upon her body. He raised his fingers to her hair and the blood fell away as if she'd just been shampooed, rinsed, and dried, and it was once again hanging in soft waves down her back.

Ares stepped back and his eyes sought Rachel's. She looked up into his smiling face. "You are now almost ready to attend the mating ceremony."

Rachel ran a hand down her body. "How can I ever thank you for this?"

"Thank me by accepting my King at the ceremony today."

Rachel's eyes locked on Ares. He was serious. He wanted nothing for himself, only the King's happiness. She grabbed him and kissed him full on the mouth. When she stepped away, she saw Ares's jade eyes widen in surprise, then his face darkened to a lovely shade of red.

Rachel's giggles turned into full on guffaws. Never would she have believed she'd be able to embarrass Ares, the fierce hunter. But the proof stood before her, blushing from head to toe, shuffling his feet.

Ares coughed. His eyes averted to the floor. "I have one more thing to do in preparation of the ceremony."

Rachel heaved in a breath and fanned her face. "What do you have to do? I thought we were done."

Ares pulled out a flask and poured the contents into a bowl. Rachel's eyes widened. "I'm not drinking that."

Ares smiled. "'Tis not for consumption."

"Then what is it?"

"A special blend of oil." His eyes never left his task. "Where would you like to have me apply it to your skin, on the bed or standing?"

"You're going to rub that on me?"

Ares's eyes flashed to hers, hot and dangerous — terrifyingly male.

Rachel licked her lips. She owed him. Her nipples pebbled tighter at the thought of his calloused hands moving over her body. The thought shouldn't turn her on, but it did, even though she had no feelings for the handsome warrior other than a blossoming friendship. She coughed, trying to alleviate the sudden dryness in her throat. Her mind scrambled to the bed furs and back.

Ares met her gaze. "Well…" He quirked an arrogant brow.

"You choose the position of application," she croaked.

Rachel heard something like a growl come from his chest. Ares stuck his hands into the amber liquid. He rubbed the oil into his palms, while he walked around behind Rachel.

He stopped a hairsbreadth away, his breath coming out in warm puffs against her bare shoulders, sending shivery sensation racing through her nerves. Rachel felt the heat emanating from his warrior's body. Her skin prickled and gooseflesh rose as if she could feel his gaze taking in her nakedness. She gulped. Her heart belonged to Eros, but she wasn't completely immune to the sexy man standing behind her.

Ares's rough palms came down on her shoulders, the sound of flesh hitting flesh ringing out in the silence of the hut. Rachel felt the jolt clear to her toes and flinched. He seemed to ignore her reaction and began to rub the citrus scented oil, massaging it in circles over her smooth skin.

"Relax," he whispered against her ear, his lips lingering on the tender flesh.

Rachel's breathing hitched.

His hands massaged down the length of her arms and then back up. He worked his way to her collarbone and neck. The rings in Rachel's nipples felt as if they were vibrating with each stroke. She closed her eyes and inhaled. She couldn't believe that such strong hands could be so gentle.

Lost in sensation, she didn't feel his fingers drift lower. The pad of a rough thumb scraped across her nipple. Rachel's eyes flew open. She tried to turn, but Ares's arms pulled her close, her bottom snuggling against his straining erection.

"Ares, I'm not...I can't...Eros." Rachel couldn't even put a coherent sentence together.

"Relax, my Queen. I'm only here to prepare you, not join," he purred. "'Tis important that you are sated before the ceremony begins. 'Tis part of the ritual, nothing more."

Ares reached up and cupped both her breasts with his large hands. It didn't feel like "nothing more" to Rachel. He squeezed her nipples, circling them, while playing with the rings. Her pussy lips grew wet and her clit twitched. Rachel moaned and all thought of resistance left her.

Ares spread the rest of the oil along her legs and over her buttocks, massaging her muscles. The urge to rut was great. The thoughts Rachel broadcast were in turmoil, her mind torn between enjoying his caresses and being ashamed by her body's response. Her mind kept racing to someone she referred to as Jac. A vision flashed in Ares's mind of long legs, tight high breasts and short blonde hair. She had a strong yet feminine face with wide blue eyes and bright red lips.

His cock hardened painfully, as he followed Rachel's wayward thoughts, bucking beneath his loincloth. She looked up to this woman for her courage and strength. Rachel considered this Jac daring and tough, trained to fight in a man's world.

He'd been confused when she'd asked herself mentally what Jac would do in this situation. Then it occurred to him she sought the woman's guidance from past experiences. He bit back the urge to laugh, recalling Eros's earlier warning.

Ariel the seer had been even more cryptic. She told him he would find what he least expected yet most desired, following the King's orders.

Ares's curiosity was piqued by this woman named Jac. He imagined what it would be like pleasuring her in the same manner as the Queen. From Rachel's thoughts and memories, he knew she'd fight like hell. He decided he would like that—a lot. Excitement filled him, flowing to his loins as he pondered his new assignment. Ares considered the challenge of taming the warrior woman. A carnal smile stole across his face as his hands found Rachel's pleasure center.

Ares held Rachel close and spread her knees slightly apart with his own. Her breath came out in gasps and she ground her hairless mound against his hand. He circled the little nub hidden beneath her folds, stroking, teasing, coaxing, and then flicked the nerve bundle with his nail, sending the new Queen over the edge. She shrieked as her orgasm rocked her.

Ares stepped a short distance away, his hand wrapped firmly around his cock, visions of Jac swimming in his head. Shuddering, he found his release, spilling his seed into his loincloth and onto the floor. Stunned by his physical reaction to Rachel's thoughts, he pulled himself together by sending an energy burst through his body. His work here was done. The Queen was now officially prepared for the ceremony.

* * * * *

Rachel stumbled toward the table and dropped into a chair, her legs too rubbery to hold her up. Her skin was flushed and slick with oil. She still couldn't believe she'd allowed Ares to bring her to orgasm. But she did owe him and if this was part of his official duties, then far be it from her to complain.

It amazed her how fast she'd gone from lecturing Jac and Brigit about the pitfalls of sexual gratification to willingly participating. *Oh, how the mighty have fallen.* Never in all her years would she have been able to predict that she, Dr. Rachel Evans, would find herself participating naked in a pagan-like ritual. Jac would have a field day with this info. Rachel shook her head, glancing down at her oiled skin, and then giggled as she imagined Jac's strangled expression.

Ares stood next to the hut entrance. His face glowed with pride. His eyes held no sign of judgment. "I will wait outside to escort you once you are dressed, my Queen. Thank you for the honor you have bestowed upon my family's house." He bowed and went out the door.

Rachel walked to the other chair and picked up the clothing. Once again, there was no top. The material was aquamarine like Eros's eyes and felt like silk. She pulled it through her fingers, luxuriating in the feel.

Rachel slipped the skirt on. The fabric draped low on her hips. She took a couple of deep breaths, then exited the hut. Ares stood on the other side of the door, his large frame blocking the branch path.

"What do you think?" Rachel twirled, sending material swirling in the air. She heard a sharp intake of breath as she came to a stop.

She smiled. "Thank you."

"My Queen, I only hope that my mate is as lovely." Ares inclined his head toward her, then stepped aside.

"Then you are not mated?"

He smiled. "No." He held out his elbow and waited for her to place her hand on his arm. He led her down the path and into the basket, lowering it quickly.

A crowd had gathered in the center of the compound. A long table had been set up on the side. Fruits, breads and fish were piled high, making it a sumptuous feast. Rachel searched the crowd, her eyes seeking Eros.

He stood next to the seer, his blond hair separated into three intricately woven braids. He wore an ocean blue sarong, almost identical to the one Rachel had been given. Gold bands encircled his muscular biceps and wrists. His head was held high and his shoulders were thrown back, exposing his massive chest. His shallow breaths sent ripples through his washboard stomach.

Rachel's breath caught. Never in her life had she gazed upon such fierce masculine beauty. Her body tingled as she considered the ramifications of this ceremony. She was binding herself to this god of a man. The thought terrified and excited her. She'd be Mrs. Eros or Dr. Rachel Evans, Queen of Atlantis. Eros's eyes met hers. They were swimming with love.

Rachel swallowed the lump in her throat. She'd settle for being Eros's woman.

"Are you ready to accept your position as Queen?" Ares asked, a mark of hesitation in his voice.

"It is all that you asked of me when you saved my life. I think it's the least I can do," she replied.

Ares stopped short, turning Rachel in his arms until she faced him. "Eros deserves more than that." Ares's eyes bore down on her with an intensity she hadn't experienced before. "Are you willing to give him all?"

Rachel knew that when she answered Ares's question, there would be no turning back. But in truth, she had no wish to go anywhere. Her place was here at Eros's side. "I love him, Ares, with all my heart. I accepted the fact the other day when Eros and I went for a walk. Last night only reinforced how important he is to me, because I came so close to losing him."

He smiled and his eyes sparkled. "'Tis good." He patted her hand. "Now let us join you to your future mate." Ares laughed. "I fear he can wait no longer."

They both turned and proceeded forward. Eros practically vibrated with leashed intensity. His orbs sought hers in assurance. Rachel smiled up at him, then turned to face the seer.

She figured the ceremony would resemble a regular wedding, but that was not the case. The seer placed her hand upon Rachel's head. She felt intense heat and then heard a loud pop. Rachel clutched her ears.

Are you all right? The seer asked without moving her lips.

"What?" Rachel stared at her for a few seconds, disoriented. This wasn't possible. She'd heard Ariel's thoughts. Her brows furrowed as reality sank in.

So you are well. The seer smiled and started the ceremony.

The vows were delivered in Atlantean as was customary, but Rachel heard and understood every word. No one told her she'd be telepathic after the ceremony or that she'd understand this new language. She wasn't sure how she felt about this gift, but figured since most of the Atlanteans spoke to each other in this manner, it was probably a good skill to have. She snorted at her staunch practicality.

The strange thing was it seemed to be more than simple telepathy. With each uttered word from the seer, Rachel's understanding of Atlantis expanded, solidified, defying all explanation. As unbelievable as it seemed, she now knew beyond a doubt these people were as they said.

The ceremony ended when Eros placed a set of matching armbands on Rachel. He dipped his head down, capturing her mouth in a searing kiss. The crowd erupted in cheers and well-wishes, as the couple turned as one. She was officially married, at least in the eyes of the Atlanteans. This was a day she'd never thought she would see. The weight of her decision hit her square in the chest and her eyes rounded as Rachel stood by Eros's side taking in the sight of the people...*her people.*

Chapter Sixteen

Eros led Rachel to the feast table. He couldn't help himself when he ran his hand along her spine, reveling in the tiny shivers he provoked. He guided Rachel to a chair toward the center of the table, pulling it out as he waited for her to be seated. She was his — all his.

She appeared to be overwhelmed by her new ability, but presented a brave face to the crowd. She didn't yet know how to tune out the endless chatter. He grabbed her hand and raised her fingers to his lips.

She shuddered, desire filling her dazzled eyes.

He took the seat next to hers and raised a cup to toast his new bride, Queen Rachel. Everyone joined in, their joy and good tidings emanated out, wrapping around the newly formed union.

Why am I so warm? Rachel thought.

'Tis just the energy from our people. They are healing and changing your primitive system. You will now age as we do and it will aid in our fertility.

You're kidding, right?

No, my Queen. By the time we leave the feast you will be ovulating and I will be potent. 'Tis the way Atlanteans guarantee procreation. His lips twitched as he fought to keep a smile from forming on his face.

Eros didn't think Rachel would find this particular item of knowledge amusing.

You mean if we have sex tonight I'm going to get pregnant? Her face drained of color.

If? He arched a brow in her direction. *You do not wish to bear my spawn?* Eros clenched his jaw and braced himself, waiting for her reply.

I...I refuse to answer that on the grounds that it might incriminate me. She crossed her arms over her chest and refused to meet his eyes. *Were you serious about the aging thing?*

Eros nodded, then burst out laughing, all tension leaving his body in a flood of emotion. He looked forward to the completion of the meal so that he could take his bride and experience what he could only before imagine. He practically growled at the thought.

Her taut breasts teased him. Her arms pushed them up, plumping them high until they all but spilled over. He caught glimpses of her rosy nipples peeking out. Eros longed to lap at them until they kernelled into tight balls. He brushed the underside of one with his knuckle. The skin puckered, begging for his touch.

Rachel's breathing hitched.

He grew hard once again thinking about finally enjoying the pleasures of her body. Eros decided that he shouldn't be the only one suffering, so he sent Rachel a very vivid picture of exactly what he planned to do to her once the celebration died down.

Her eyes darted from side to side, before meeting his head on. She squirmed in her seat. Her cheeks flushed a lovely shade of pink. *How could you embarrass me in front of your people?*

Our people cannot hear what I am saying to you or showing you. I have used what you would call a private line, to contact you.

"Oh," she said aloud, her shoulders slumping in relief.

Eros slid his hand along her leg until he reached the juncture of her woman's center.

"Don't do that," she chastised breathlessly. Her eyes sparked, but with a different kind of fire.

No one can see us. The table conceals my actions. He trailed his fingers over her thigh until he reached her clit. Rachel's skin flushed and she looked about the table at the other party revelers' faces. Eros began a slow, lazy massage through her skirt. The material only added to the friction as he followed Rachel's thoughts.

A slow grin spread across his face. *If you cry out they will know what we've been doing.*

Rachel looked at Eros, then down at the table. She bit on her lower lip to keep from moaning aloud. Her pussy throbbed and her nipples marbled. She couldn't believe she'd allowed him to do this to her at their reception dinner.

She was convinced jungle fever had taken over her system and transformed her into a different person, a wild exhibitionist that held no ounce of shame and lived only for hedonistic thrills. Eros continued his probing, all the while having conversations with the various men at the table.

Rachel felt the pressure building. As if on cue, Eros intensified his movements, pressing on her clit, sending her over the edge. Light flashed behind her eyelids. Blood pounded in her ears. Before she could cry out he captured her mouth in a scorching kiss, drowning all sound. His hungry lips devoured her, demanding the same in return. Rachel gave him everything she had, her body pulsing in release.

When she'd finally floated back to reality, she realized he hadn't played fair. *See what he thinks of this.* Rachel bit her lip and conjured the most erotic picture she could of her naked, riding his mighty cock, her head thrown back, her hair tickling his thighs, nipples jutting as one hand reached back to caress his balls, while the other dug into the flesh at his abdomen. She sent the image to Eros or at least she hoped she had.

For a moment nothing happened, then slowly his facial expression changed from jovial to tense. He shifted in his seat, tugging at his sarong. Red tinged his high cheekbones and he couldn't seem to swallow the food he'd taken a bite of for his jaw seemed locked in place.

Rachel giggled and looked straight ahead. She could feel his heated gaze upon her, at any moment she expected her clothes to burst into flames.

The party's volume rose. Food was playfully tossed into waiting mouths, the innocent act a strange kind of Atlantean foreplay. With the bounty consumed, women and men began to clear the table.

A fire was built up in the center of the village. Men brought out various musical instruments, some resembling flutes, others guitars, and began to play. The melody remained light and airy, almost dreamlike in its depth until two men approached carrying drums.

Primal, forbidden, the beat began luring everyone into the circle with promises of pleasure.

The Atlantean women shed their clothing and began a slow seductive dance around the fire in time to the primitive pulse. They fondled their breasts, displaying their prominent nipples to the men's eager faces. Swaying their rounded hips enticingly, they bent over, spread their pussy lips, and began to fondle their clits.

The music intensified and so did their movements. They became animalistic, dropping to the ground, reaching for the night sky. Calling down the moon. One by one they reached orgasm.

Women approached other women, rubbing their bodies together and taking turns licking and kissing each other's nipples until they pebbled. Sweat beaded their bodies. Flame reflected off their heated skin, lighting the trail of moisture left behind by greedy mouths. Eyes glazed, the men watched with intense interest, their shouts blending with the carnal frenzy.

The seer stood statue-like on the sidelines, rubbing her cunt with oil. Her body glistened. Ariel's head was thrown back in ecstasy like an enchanted goddess. When the wetness between her thighs was apparent for all to see, she joined the performance, her perfect body rotating to the music like a consummate harem girl. She paused before a handsome blond warrior on the other side, gyrating and spreading her thighs to expose her clit to his hungry eyes.

"Who is that?" Rachel pointed to the man.

"That is Coridan," Eros snorted. "He is a youth that shows great promise, if he can learn how to control his temper. In truth, he's much like Ares." Eros smiled. "The seer loves to tease."

"I can see that." Rachel laughed. Coridan's erection was discernable from the other side of the clearing.

Ariel continued on, twirling and dancing, until she found Cassandra, one of the women Rachel had spoken to yesterday. Ariel gently lowered her to the ground, trailing kisses from the woman's mouth to her toes. Cassandra's body undulated like a charmer taming a snake under the seer's touch. Energy glowed from her pores, turning Cassandra golden.

Ariel dropped between the woman's knees and spread her wide. She pushed the woman's skirt out of the way, until her dripping pussy lips were visible to the royal couple and the crowd. The men crept closer, the outline of their hard cocks clearly visible beneath their loincloths. She spread Cassandra's petals, exposing her engorged clit. Ariel's eyes met Rachel's, a second before she stuck out her six inch tongue and disappeared between Cassandra's thighs.

The seer lapped at Cassandra's pussy like a woman possessed. She swirled around her clit, plunging deep into her channel, tongue fucking the woman. Moments later Cassandra let out a scream of release. The energy within her burst forth, giving off an almost blinding light. Little growling noises emanated from Ariel's throat, letting the woman know exactly how much she enjoyed pleasuring her.

Rachel shifted and felt herself growing wet as she watched the strange mating ritual from Eros's side. She couldn't help but wonder what it would be like to have the seer buried between her thighs. Rachel's breathing dropped to a deep cadence, her breasts quivering with each exhale, vibrating the rings on her nipples. She'd always considered herself so vanilla when it came to sex.

She'd never experienced voyeurism and was shocked at how titillating it could be watching two women devour each other in such an uninhibited way. She swallowed hard and crossed her legs to ease the steady throb.

I can smell your arousal, my Queen. You find it exciting to watch the seer?

"N-no," Rachel squirmed, shaking her head in denial.

Eros just smiled and wet his lips.

Rachel reached for a cup of water and raised it to her dry mouth.

Ariel continued to pleasure Cassandra until the woman cried out her third orgasm, then the seer rose and wiped her face with the back of her hand. Her lustful eyes sought Rachel's once again and she smiled, bowing low, before retreating to her hut.

"Does Ariel have someone waiting for her?" Rachel pointed to the dwelling.

Eros shook his head. "The seer cannot join with another. It would diminish her powers."

"She can't have sex?" Rachel sucked in a breath. *Talk about frustration.*

"No," he crossed his arms over his wide chest. "Not while the portal is closed."

After following the seer's retreat with his aqua gaze, Coridan, the Atlantean man Rachel had inquired about earlier, dropped to his knees to pick up where Ariel left off. He ripped away his loincloth, releasing his massive erection. Cassandra's head writhed from side to side as he buried his thick cock in her wet channel, her screams signaling another release. Coridan drove into Cassandra, plunging in and out of her pussy like a battering ram, his body flexing and straining.

Rachel uncrossed her legs and stared spellbound at the Bacchanalia taking place before her. She tried not to stare at the young warrior's nicely rounded ass as he continued to fuck Cassandra.

One by one the people of Atlantis began to pair up. Some women rode the men as if trying to break in a wild horse, their excited cries echoing through the trees, while others sought feminine company, their faces happily buried in each others cunts lapping away, teasing clits until they vibrated on the ground. A few had taken two warriors at the side of the fire. While one fucked their pussy the other pinched and kissed their nipples, nibbling on the clits, coaxing the women to take their cocks deeper into their throats. When relief was reached, they'd switch positions. The women were constantly filled on both ends.

Rachel had been so taken in by the performance she almost missed Coridan's retreat to the far side of the clearing. He now ignored the festivities and stared at Ares. His arms crossed over his massive chest, aqua eyes sparking fire.

"What's with Coridan?" Rachel pointed to the other side of the fire. Eros followed her finger, then shrugged.

"Why is he staring at Ares like that, instead of participating some more?" Her brows furrowed and she glanced at Ares, who didn't seem to be paying attention to the man.

"They have a friendly rivalry going on between them, always trying to out do one another." Eros sounded bored as if the situation had been taking place for so long it was now tiresome. "Mayhap he is waiting to see if Ares favors a woman, before Coridan makes his move for her. 'Tis harmless."

Rachel shook her head. Men...*Some things never change*. She'd take Eros's word for the rivalry, but Coridan didn't look harmless to her.

Ares sat off to the side, his eyes lazily taking in the performance. Rachel could see his erection buck beneath his loincloth with each thrust the men around the fire made, but the dark hunter made no move to encourage any of the dancing women. For a second his gaze met Coridan's. There was a flash of challenge before Ares's lips kicked up in a smile.

"Why doesn't Ares pick a woman and pair up for the night?" Rachel wondered aloud as she watched several women attempt to catch the warrior's jade eyes.

Eros's gaze flicked to his friend and then back to the orgy. "He awaits his mate."

"Is she coming?"

"The seer says 'tis so."

Rachel tilted her head, surprised. "When?"

"Soon." Eros said vaguely, then grabbed Rachel's hand, pulled her up from her seat, and led her to the transport basket. "'Tis time we complete the mating ritual. Enough time has been wasted."

Chapter Seventeen

Butterflies swam in Rachel's stomach, yet at the same time she was thrilled. She was so turned on from the revelry that she didn't think she could wait another minute. It wasn't like she'd never been with a man before, but this seemed different—special. Part of her felt skittish, almost innocent.

"Come." Eros led Rachel to the hut door and moved aside the fur.

The room was illuminated by candles, giving it a soft glow. Fresh mangos, bananas and camu camu were placed in a bowl on the table. Orchids and lilies were in various carved vases around the small hut, the scent sweet and invigorating. Juice had been left in jugs so that the newlyweds wouldn't have to leave the hut for days.

Eros dropped the door covering once she'd stepped inside. His hands shook as he reached out to trace a finger over her shoulder, stopping at her collarbone. The light touch sent shivers skipping through Rachel's body. Her nipples peaked, then ached, her body yearning for more contact. Her breathing deepened, growing choppy with anticipation. She was already wet from watching the various couplings. Her pussy demanded relief in the form of his massive cock.

"I will go as slow as you wish, my Queen." Eros took a deep calming breath. "Tell me what you want."

"I w-want." Her voice cracked. "I want you."

Eros wrapped his arms around her, drawing her against his warm body. His lips touched her forehead, then he kissed her eyes and nose. He bypassed her mouth and sought out the pulse point along her vulnerable throat. He nipped and pecked until he reached her earlobe. He sucked it between his teeth, licking and placing small bites around the shell of her ear.

Rachel mewled. She wanted more, much more. She pulled back. Eros's eyes were glazed over with passion. She grabbed his hand and led him to the bed of furs. Rachel pulled on the material of her sarong until it dropped to the floor. Her small hands wrapped around his throbbing cock through the matching material.

"Finally, I get to feel you inside me." She moved her hands tentatively up and down.

Fire flared from Eros, turning his aqua orbs molten. He sucked in a ragged breath and closed his eyes. "You are going to kill me, my Queen, if you keep up this tender torture."

Rachel laughed, but didn't drop her hands. She tugged, removing his clothing, then leaned forward and took Eros in her mouth. She could barely wrap her lips around his girth, although she loved pleasuring him this way. He was large. So big in fact, she was pretty sure there was no way he'd fit inside her…at least not all of him.

He stroked her hair. "I have dreamed about this moment," he said, a bit breathless. "I have waited so long."

Rachel stilled, recalling her own dreams. Then she smiled and sucked on him, running her tongue along the tip. He bucked in her mouth. His pre-cum tasted salty, sweet, and delicious. Rachel continued working his cock, reveling in the feel of his satiny hardness, until Eros pulled her away.

"'Tis my turn." He laid her on the bed.

Eros fought the urge to rut inside her. She needed to be prepared for his entry. He sank to the floor and carefully spread her legs apart, enjoying the beauty of her flowering petals. She smelled musky and perfect, all woman — his woman. His mouth watered at the thought of tasting her pussy again.

He dipped his head. Her juices flowed from her, whetting his appetite. Eros found her clit and began working it with his tongue and teeth until it became engorged. Rachel's head thrashed back and forth on the furs and her legs trembled. Her cries grew in volume as she reached her first of many peaks.

Eros rose up and positioned himself at her entrance. He debated whether to tell Rachel that she was once again a virgin, due to the healing energy the people had put forth at the celebration table. He decided against it. All the waiting, yearning, overwhelming need to join had culminated to this one moment. They were both too far gone. Some things were best left to experience.

Rachel felt pressure as Eros entered her. He had only just pushed the tip in, yet she felt stretched beyond belief. Was she that nervous about the wedding night that she'd tensed? Rachel didn't think so. She'd just had an orgasm, if anything it should ease his way. She took a deep breath. This wasn't going to work.

"Shh, I will fit, just relax," he murmured through gritted teeth. Sweat broke out on Eros's brow as he strained to maintain control as he inched in.

He slid a tiny bit further before being stopped by her woman's barrier. Rachel's breath caught. It wasn't possible. She'd lost her virginity back in high school in the backseat of a Chevy on Prom night. She remembered because it had been such an unpleasant experience.

"H-How?" Her brows furrowed.

"The feast. I'm sorry," he groaned out a second before he thrust forward, impaling Rachel.

She screamed. The breath left her body as the pain of being re-deflowered shot through her. Eros rested above her, his weight transferred to his elbows, so that she could breathe.

"Are you all right, my Rachel? Speak to me." He brushed the hair away from her face.

The pain started to ebb, along with the shock. Rachel felt full, tight, overflowing. Eros drew out of her halfway before making a slow thrust forward. His massive cock, so big, so filling — so encompassing. Sensation started to build within her as he rocked into her again. The fire spread through her limbs to her nipples, until they throbbed.

Rachel clenched her legs around his hips. "I'm all right now." He thrust, scorching her silken vice. "Don't stop!"

His cock pulsed inside her with each roll of his hips, sweeping her senses, gauging her need. Rachel felt an unfamiliar tension build inside — more powerful than she'd ever experienced before. Her heart thudded madly in anticipation, as her body trembled with feverish need. She brought her feet down and slanted her hips to ease his access in her drenched pussy. Eros increased his speed, stabbing and stroking, merging and plunging. He wrapped his legs around hers, locking her in place, his thrusts growing more frantic. His cock surged, nudging her womb.

Rachel's body shuddered and she came, biting his shoulder as the sensations got to be too much. She threw her head back, a shriek of pleasure escaping from her throat. Eros latched onto her mouth, burying her cry beneath his lips in a searing embrace. He kissed her deep, his tongue matching the motion of his driving hips. Eros broke the kiss and stilled his movements. His eyes sought out Rachel's.

"What?" Rachel said mindlessly, unable to focus. "Don't stop," she pleaded, her nails digging into the skin of his taut back.

"Will you accept my seed into your womb?"

She frowned, her body arching beneath him. "W-Wha?"

"Will you accept me?" His voice was savage, yet vulnerable.

Rachel gazed into his eyes and gladly leapt into their blue depths. "Yes," she cried.

Eros's muscles bunched and his face tightened. He thrust forward sheathing himself to the hilt. Eros felt his sac draw up a second before his cock pulsed, spilling its seed. He groaned, as her pussy milked him, his hips involuntarily pumping until the last drop left his body. Sweat coated their bodies as each labored for breath.

Still joined, he pulled Rachel close to him, until she snuggled against his chest. Eros felt his cock begin to harden once again, as energy pulsed through him. Rachel's eyes widened in surprise before she smiled, then her tongue darted out to wet her lower lip. Eros angled his head, kissing her gently at first, before turning up the heat.

He bucked his hips, sending his shaft deeper into her core. He swallowed the gasp that escaped from her lips.

"You can't be ready to go again," she giggled, tossing her hair over her shoulder.

He raised a brow and stared into her sated face. "What do you think?"

She burst out laughing. "I think I've discovered a monster."

Eros rolled, bringing Rachel with him, until she was seated on top, straddling him. "I want you to ride me like the women were doing around the campfire." He nudged his hips, enough to draw out a moan from her swollen lips.

Rachel slid her fingers over the expanse of his chest, reveling in the muscles beneath her palms. The warmth of his smooth skin, the flat pierced discs that made up his male nipples, and the rock hard cock buried in her body. Like a piece of Michelangelo's marble come to life, this man was every woman's fantasy, yet he was all hers. Only hers. She smiled again, this time wider.

She rose up an inch or two, then sank down, feeling his thick length slide back inside of her drenched pussy. The sensation of taking in his massive cock was powerful, intimidating—addictive. She didn't think she'd ever tire of feeling him hard and pulsing inside of her. Rachel leaned forward releasing even more of his erection from her velvet grip. She closed her eyes for a second, relishing the feel of the hard steel searing her cunt.

Rachel captured his gaze and then picked up speed. His eyes bore into her, watching her every move. Her nipples bounced, sending the gold rings flopping against her skin. Eros seemed mesmerized. Rachel kept her smile to herself, exalting in the power she wielded over this mighty warrior king. Her pussy sucked him deeper while her clit scraped over the crisp curls at the base of his cock. She groaned, allowing the feeling to sweep over her, radiating out.

Eros bent his head forward, capturing her nipple. His tongue swirled and flicked. Rachel ground her clit into his body, so close to release. It was Eros's turn to moan. He gripped her waist, lifting her tired body up and down onto his hard shaft as his hips rose up to meet her. Rachel shrieked as her orgasm slammed her violently. Her body trembled and shook as her vaginal walls pulsed, locking onto Eros's cock like a vise. It was enough to send him spiraling after her. His essence jettisoned out filling her, joining them. She collapsed forward onto his chest.

"I love you," Rachel rasped, her voice sated and sleepy.

He drew her to his side, tucking her beneath his shoulder. "I love you, too." He placed one hand protectively over her abdomen. Their unborn child now grew inside her. She had saved his people. Saved him.

Eros sighed, content for the moment. If only it were that simple. His people still had a long journey ahead, fraught with many perils before reaching their final destination—before they could go home.

The End

Coming soon...

"Atlantean's Quest Book Two: Exodus"

Jac will need more than the pistols strapped to her hips to protect her when she journeys down to the jungle to rescue her friend Rachel. She's about to come face-to-face with her greatest sexual fear…a man she can call her *equal*.

Join Jac as she pulls out her entire feminine arsenal in an attempt to avoid a heat-seeking missile known as Ares.

About the author:

Jordan Summers is a no-nonsense Midwesterner with a romantic streak a mile wide. Happily-ever-after is a must whether she's at the movies or enjoying a good book.

Jordan wrote her first romance in high school and will be forever grateful to the creative writing teacher who encouraged her overactive imagination.

Just as at home on a ranch as she is in a major city, Jordan now lives out West. She enjoys spending time with her husband, the definition of a romantic renaissance man, going to bookstores, and visiting family and friends in Scotland.

Jordan Summers welcomes mail from readers. You can write to them c/o Ellora's Cave Publishing at P.O. Box 787, Hudson, Ohio 44236-0787.

Why an electronic book?

We live in the Information Age—an exciting time in the history of human civilization in which technology rules supreme and continues to progress in leaps and bounds every minute of every hour of every day. For a multitude of reasons, more and more avid literary fans are opting to purchase e-books instead of paperbacks. The question to those not yet initiated to the world of electronic reading is simply: *why?*

1. *Price.* An electronic title at Ellora's Cave Publishing runs anywhere from 40-75% less than the cover price of the <u>exact same title</u> in paperback format. Why? Cold mathematics. It is less expensive to publish an e-book than it is to publish a paperback, so the savings are passed along to the consumer.

2. *Space.* Running out of room to house your paperback books? That is one worry you will never have with electronic novels. For a low one-time cost, you can purchase a handheld computer designed specifically for e-reading purposes. Many e-readers are larger than the average handheld, giving you plenty of screen room. Better yet, hundreds of titles can be stored within your new library—a single microchip. (Please note that Ellora's Cave does not endorse any specific brands. You can check our website at *www.ellorascave.com*

for customer recommendations we make available to new consumers.)

3. *Mobility.* Because your new library now consists of only a microchip, your entire cache of books can be taken with you wherever you go.

4. *Personal preferences are accounted for.* Are the words you are currently reading too small? Too large? Too…**ANNOYING**? Paperback books cannot be modified according to personal preferences, but e-books can.

5. *Innovation.* The *way* you read a book is not the only advancement the Information Age has gifted the literary community with. There is also the factor of *what* you can read. Ellora's Cave Publishing will be introducing a new line of interactive titles that are available in e-book format only.

6. *Instant gratification.* Is it the middle of the night and all the bookstores are closed? Are you tired of waiting days—sometimes weeks—for online and offline bookstores to ship the novels you bought? Ellora's Cave Publishing sells instantaneous downloads 24 hours a day, 7 days a week, 365 days a year. Our e-book delivery system is 100% automated, meaning your order is filled as soon as you pay for it.

Those are a few of the top reasons why electronic novels are displacing paperbacks for many an avid reader. As always, Ellora's Cave Publishing welcomes your questions and comments. We invite you to email us at service@ellorascave.com or write to us directly at: P.O. Box 787, Hudson, Ohio 44236-0787.

Printed in the United States
19818LVS00006B/67-93